NORDIC & FINN

ALSO BY PETER BRANDVOLD

NORDIC & FINN

NORDIC & FINN
BOOK ONE

PETER BRANDVOLD

WOLFPACK
PUBLISHING
— EST 2013 —

Nordic & Finn
Paperback Edition
Copyright © 2024 Peter Brandvold

Wolfpack Publishing
1707 E. Diana Street
Tampa, FL 33609

wolfpackpublishing.com

Paperback ISBN 978-1-63977-560-6
eBook ISBN 978-1-63977-559-0
LCCN 2024941987

NORDIC & FINN

CHAPTER ONE

Anders Nordic was a big, bearded Norwegian American from Dakota Territory who owned a set of eyes so blue most people described them as startling, even chilling.

Not eyes you wanted staring at you. They peered out of a broad, chiseled face some described as forbidding, with broad, high-tapering cheekbones and a full mouth inside a thick beard the color of north country wheat. Today, the taciturn loner walked out the Burns & Peterson Mercantile in Cimarron, New Mexico Territory, with a set of bulging panniers slung over his shoulders some described as broad as a yoke.

They were not shoulders you wanted confronting you in a saloon or anywhere else, nor were his hands, the size of butt roasts, did you want threatening you with a smack to the jaw.

The big, moody Dakotan paused, scowled at the heavy traffic on the street before him—the congested, teeming wash of humanity, the thunder of wagons, men's yells and shouts, and the rataplan of horse and mule hooves—and descended the steps to the street. He strapped the panniers to his beefy dun packhorse already outfitted with two other sets of the bulging, freshly filled packs—enough stores to get him through another month in the mountains.

At least, he hoped.

Anders Nordic, a solitary soul who'd rarely gotten along with others—not even when he'd been a young lad growing up on his family's farm in Dakota Territory—hated coming to town worse than almost anything. No, he hated coming to town more than anything. What Anders liked were the long, quiet days of slow, deliberate toil in the mountains, and the even longer, somnolent nights repairing harness or reading by a crackling fire, hearing nothing more than the coyotes and wolves yammering on the ridges looming over the line shack he currently occupied near the Chama River in northern New Mexico's Chama Mountains.

That's what Anders Nordic did, had been doing since he was twenty-three years old. Now thirty-four, he continued working for ranchers, guarding their far-flung summer herds in remote mountain line shacks from southern New Mexico to northern Colorado's Never Summer Range. It was the work he'd been born to do. He'd tried to punch cattle, but that meant working with other men, and being brusque, idiosyncratic, and downright antisocial, that had never gone well for Anders.

Or for the men who'd worked with him.

For some reason, most men were herd-like follow-ers. They didn't seem to cotton to men best described as "herd quitters"—men others deemed "different," who didn't say much and preferred to keep to them-selves. The herd followers disliked the herd quitters even more when those "different" others were big and imposing, with anvil-like shoulders and hamlike hands. They saw them as threatening partly due to their size. And Anders, at six foot four and broad as a barn door, was far outsized by most other men's standards.

For that reason, when he'd been living in a bunkhouse for more than a few days, one or more of the other cowpunchers' noses or arms or legs or ribs had ended up broken and Anders had either been fired or jailed. Sometimes both. Both things were hard on a man's poke not to mention his patience. So now Anders confined his work to remote line shacks where he lived alone, sometimes with a stray dog or cat or even, now and then, a raccoon or two. Once, he'd even had a pet badger he'd named Lenore, after his mother, one of the few people in this world he'd felt a kinship to.

Anders liked animals. Not people. If he could live alone in the world with no other people but just animals, he'd wake up grinning and go to sleep the same. As it was, his heavy brows were usually ridged, his keen blue eyes dark and brooding, his mouth downturned at the corners inside his shaggy, blond beard, as they were now, having had to endure another trip to town to restock his remote cabin's larder.

Now, however, he'd paid his bill at the mercantile, and his supplies were secured to his packhorse. He could head back into the mountains straightaway, but he had one more stop to make. That was a saloon aptly named the Who Hit John, because the Taos lightning they served would make John or anyone who imbibes feel the next few hours like they were hit over the head with a sledgehammer and dragged into an alley to die a slow, agonizing death.

But Anders brewed his own beer up in his cabin, and the brewer at the Who Hit John, Barnabas McNulty, brewed a nice ale for which he grew his own hops. It was this hops that Anders bought from McNulty. So, when he swung up on the back of his rangy Appaloosa, Apache, as he'd named the prized stallion after the one people he respected, he booted him on up the street, leading by its hackamore rope the packhorse, Angus, named after the lone uncle he'd been able to tolerate growing up.

As he angled toward the opposite side of the street after letting pass a big ore dray drawn by six mules being cursed at by the scrawny, ugly, girlish-voiced driver, he saw three kids that would barely rise to Anders's belt buckle tease a scruffy-looking collie dog with a long, slender snout and shaggy, unkempt black-and-white fur. One of the boys, a redhead with pinched up, mean eyes, was prodding the dog with a stick, poking at it like a picador, yelling and dancing and tossing his other hand in the air. The nasty kid was having a high old time at the dog's expense. The dog fought back, barking, growling, and trying to grab the stick. Anders could tell the dog was deeply frustrated, and who wouldn't be? Those vermin shavers probably teased that dog every day. It was probably high sport to them, making the miserable life of the poor dog, likely a stray, one of many in town, even more miserable than it would have been without the taunting.

"Hey, you urchins," Anders's voice thundered above the din of the street, "leave that dog alone or I'll hold all three of you down and let him bite your ears off!"

The three urchins turned to Nordic with belligerent looks. The redhead appeared as though he were about to spout back something sassy. But then his dung-brown eyes surveyed Anders's tall, bulky, bearded frame. They grew wide and then he dropped the stick and backed away, hang-jawed, as did the other two, before they swung around and ran as though they were sure the big blond Norski from Dakota was about to cook them in a cauldron of boiling pig's blood.

Which, at the moment, the hot-blooded Dakotan would love to do.

The dog looked at Anders, mewled, then headed into a near alley mouth where it slinked under a slanting jumble of packing crates.

"Poor critter," Anders said, putting his horses up to the hitchrack fronting the Who Hit John. "That devilish little redhead should be the one livin' under those crates."

He swung down from Apache's back, tied both

horses to the rack, mounted the boardwalk, hitched his denim trousers, the cuffs of which were tucked into the tops of his high, brown leather boots, higher on his hips. He adjusted the bone-gripped, long-barreled .44 Colt revolver he wore high on his right thigh in defense of men—mainly, rustlers up where he was lodged—and the occasional stalking wolf or mountain lion. In addition, he carried an 1866 Winchester repeater, or "Yellowboy," in a soft leather buckskin sheath strapped to Apache's saddle. On his broad upper torso, he wore a soft, cream cambric tunic and a colorful orange-and-yellow neckerchief with long tails.

His head was topped with a bullet-crowned, weather-stained, cream felt *sombrero*, its horsehair thong hanging loosely from around his stout, golden-tanned neck to dangle against the neckerchief tails on his chest. On his left hip, opposite the hogleg, was sheathed a Green River knife he'd made long ago when he had access to a rancher's blacksmith shop—in return for the beer he brewed and which the rancher had become partial to.

Now he pushed through the batwings, took a single, cautious glance around the shadowy drinking cave, noting a dozen or so other clients occupying tables or bellying up to the bar. There was a midafternoon, desultory air about the place that smelled of bad whiskey, good beer, and cigarette and cigar smoke as well as the sweat of hardworking men. The bar was on Anders's left. He headed for it, glad to see the apron he bought his hops from just then pulling one of the man's crisp, malty ales from a spigot poking up from a beer barrel. McNulty kept his barreled beer cold in his cellar with ice cut the previous winter.

"Ah, Mr. Nordic," said the short, stout, bearded Barnabas McNulty, slamming his small, fat, work-calloused hand down on the mahogany in salute. In a heavy Scottish accent, he said, "Been awhile, my friend. How are the mountains treatin' you? Bloody well, I take it."

"They'd treat me a lot better," Anders said, if I could make another batch of ale. He winked and grinned inside his heavy beard. "For that, I need hops."

"You're in luck! I just harvested some. I'll go back and fill you a bag. You want a beer while you're wait-in'?" It was the barman's turn to grin and wink. "Fresh batch, good 'n hoppy, too—just how you like it."

"Don't mind if I do." Anders lifted his nose and sniffed the aroma wafting over a Dutch door in the wall behind the bar. "Say, is that venison stew, I smell?"

Again, the barman grinned. "Venison and a fat rattlesnake I killed under my porch. Sort of mellows the deer's gaminess. Care for a bowl? I'll throw it in free with the hops."

Anders slapped a big paw down on the bar. "Can't pass up a deal like that. Say, you got any bones with a little meat left on 'em?"

McNulty shrugged. "Oh, I might be able to fish one out of the scrap bucket. Why?"

"Fetch me a bone an' draw me a beer—will ya, McNult?"

The apron chuckled. "You got it, my big friend."

McNulty disappeared into the kitchen flanking the bar and returned a minute later with a stout deer bone still packed with marrow. It was the upper part of a leg of a big deer. He handed it over the bar to Anders, who said, "Much obliged, my friend."

While McNulty headed over to the beer spigot, Anders swung around and headed back out onto the boardwalk. He swung left, tramped over to the mouth of the alley in which the stray collie dog had disappeared, and crouched to stare into the gap between the wall of the grocery store and the leaning stack of packing crates. The collie dog lay inside the gap, roughly six feet back from the front, well hidden in the shadows. The dog lay facing Anders, its long snout resting on its front, white paws. It had been asleep, secure in its hiding place, but now it lifted its head, opened its eyes, and pricked its ears.

Seeing Anders, it lifted its hackles and showed its fine, white teeth likely cleaned and sharpened by many rabbit and gopher bones. This fella was a hunter, Anders could tell. Probably hung around town for the company of others like himself and to raid trash heaps under cover of darkness.

But, like Nordic himself, his real home was the tall an' uncut...

"Easy, boy," Anders said. "I'm friendly." He held up the heavy bone nearly as big around as his own forearm. "Look what I brought you?" He chucked the bone into the gap. It landed near the dog's front paws. The dog's hackles went down and, giving a whining yip of eagerness, grabbed the bone between its paws and went to work, hungrily gnawing it, growling his satisfaction.

Nordic chuckled, straightened, and returned to the Who Hit John and the malty ale and big, wooden bowl of venison and rattlesnake stew waiting for him, steaming beautifully, atop the bar. He didn't see McNulty. The barman was probably out back in his hops garden, filling a sack with his fragrant flowers.

Anders bellied up to the bar, drew a deep breath rife with the succulent aromas of the nicely spiced stew bearing large, dark chunks of venison and the white disks of sliced rattlesnake. Nordic cooked and ate a lot of both meats himself, but it was nice to eat someone else's now and then, which he rarely did. After the first few forkfuls, he decided to count the barman, McNulty, among the few people he could tolerate.

He'd washed half the stew down with half the dimpled schooner of rich, dark ale, when he heard the batwing doors squawk open behind him. In the backbar mirror, he watched a small, red-mustached man in a three-piece suit be led into the Who Hit John by the scrawny, ugly little redheaded viper who'd been teasing the collie dog with a stick. They were both followed into the saloon by a beefy man in his late twenties wearing a five-pointed, brass-plated star on his brown leather vest. He had one hand closed over the grips of the .45 holstered low on his right hip, gunfighter style, and he moved with a self-important swagger.

The little, redheaded viper turned toward the bar, saw Anders in the backbar mirror, and threw up an arm and pointing finger. "There he is, Pa. That's the big galoot who said he was gonna hold me down and let that wild cur chew my *ears* off!"

CHAPTER TWO

T he boy's dapper, little father with a thick, red walrus mustache too big for his face, and long, red sideburns, threw up his own arm and pointed his own accusing finger at Anders.

"You, there. I say, you there, you big ape! How dare you speak to my son like that!" He placed both hands on the boy's shoulders, protectively. "Do you know who I *am*?"

Nordic laughed at the silly little man's display, nearly spewing his last mouthful of beer at the backbar mirror. The arrogant little tinhorn was so much a part of the sickening wash of arrogant humanity congesting what would have been a much better world without it. Anders turned from the bar, running a sleeve of his tunic across his bearded mouth and said, "I wouldn't know you from Adam's off ox, mister." He strode slowly toward the little man and his redheaded demon spawn and the thuggish-looking man still standing in front of the batwings.

The thuggish man's five-pointed star identified him as a Cimarron deputy town marshal.

"And I don't care *who* you are," Anders added.

The boy's eyes widened fearfully as Nordic's large shadow slid over him and his father. The demon spawn shifted his weight from one foot to the other as though he were about to bolt.

"The boy was teasing a harmless, homeless dog with a stick out of pure meanness. Tell me why I shouldn't stomp his devilish little head into the floor until he looks more like a crushed tomato than a nasty kid!"

"Ahhh!" the boy cried, staring in horror at the big, bearded man hulking before him.

"Hey there, you!" the deputy piped up, taking one step toward Anders, who stood several inches taller than he. "This man just happens to own the Stockman's Bank of Cimarron. You'll show respect to him as well as his boy, mister, or you'll be spendin' the night in the lockup!"

Anders turned to him, rage bubbling up inside him. He clenched his hands into tight fists at his sides. "And who's gonna do that? *You?*"

"Damn right, *me!*" said the indignant deputy, taking one more step forward. "You apologize to this boy and his father, and I'll let you go."

Nordic stomped his foot and sent a guttural laugh blasting toward the ceiling. "That's a good one. I like that one. Now leave me alone so I can finish my meal in peace!"

Anders swung around and returned to the bar

behind which Barnabas McNulty stood, hands on the mahogany to each side of the burlap pouch of hops he'd set there, looking a little constipated. "How much do I owe ya, McNult?" He tipped back his glass, finishing his ale in two deep drafts.

"Two bits for the ale and the hops. Stew's on the house."

"That sounds like a good deal to me." Anders fished around in a pocket of his denims then tossed two dimes and a nickel onto the bar.

Behind him, he heard the little banker hiss, "Do something, you fool!"

In the backbar mirror he watched the deputy move toward the bar, drawing the .45 from the holster on his right thigh. "All right, mister. You're under arrest."

Anders picked up the pouch of hops and turned to the deputy, chuckling his incredulity. "I am, am I? What for?"

"Um…for…for…"

"For threatening my boy with physical violence and insulting me, one of your *betters*, you uncouth Nordic *bear*!" finished the little man for the deputy, rising up on the toes of his brown leather brogans.

"Yeah," the deputy said. "What he said!"

"Oh, for pity's sake." Before Anders could stop himself—he knew he should stop himself, but as always, he couldn't stop himself, reacting more out of instinct and emotion than reason—he thrust up the hand holding the hops pouch, knocking the deputy's gun out of the man's hand and slamming his right, clenched fist soundly against the man's face.

The man's nose turned sideways, exploding like a ripe tomato.

The deputy bellowed miserably and turned away, clutching his nose with both hands then dropping to his knees, howling.

The redheaded little demon spawn looked up at his father eagerly, yelling, "What're you gonna do, Pa? What're you gonna do?"

It was the banker's turn to look constipated.

As Nordic, chuckling, stepped around the howling deputy and moved toward the batwings, the little banker stepped around his son and ran up to him, pulling his little, pale, clenched right fist behind his right shoulder then swinging it forward and up toward Anders's face.

"Oh, for pity's sake," Anders said again, grabbing the banker's fist in his right hand and twisting it.

The little banker yipped like a whipped dog, stretched his lips back from his ridiculously mustached mouth, and dropped to his knees. "No, please… lemme…lemme go, lemme *goooo*! You'll *break* it!"

"Pa!" cried his demon child, gazing in bright-eyed terror at Anders and stumbling back against the player piano behind him, causing the piano to kick up a bizarre cacophony.

Now both the little banker and the thuggish deputy were down, howling, the deputy clutching his bloody nose, the banker holding his injured fist to his chest like a little bird with a broken wing.

Nordic sighed then pushed through the batwings. He dropped the hops bag into a saddlebag pouch on

Apache's back then unlooped both horses' reins from the hitchrack.

"I'm gonna have to stop comin' to town so often, Apache," he told the horse as he swung heavily up onto the Appaloosa's back. "Too much trouble, I tell ya. Folks is just too gallblasted much trouble!"

Holding the packhorse's reins in his right hand, he began to back Apache out away from the hitchrack. He stopped suddenly when he saw the shaggy, black-and-white collie dog sitting on the boardwalk fronting the Who Hit John. The dog was staring expectantly toward Anders, thumping his tail against the worn, gray boards.

Nordic leaned forward against his saddle horn. "You enjoyed that deer bone, didja?" He chuckled. "Whaddya think, Finn? You as ready to get out of this Sodom and Gomorrah as I am?"

The dog yipped, rose, and trotted out into the street beside Nordic and Apache, gazing up at the big man expectantly, uncertainly, shifting his weight from one front foot to the other, mewling. Anders tossed his head to indicate the packhorse standing just off Apache's right hip. "Jump up on Angus's back, Finn—kick back an' enjoy the ride back to the tall an' uncut. We got a ways to go!"

As the shaggy dog hesitated before suddenly leaping up onto the packhorse's back, Anders realized he'd already named the dog after a tinker who used to frequent his family farm in Dakota and taught Anders how to make knives. Finn Kavanaugh had been the Irishman's name, a boisterous prankster and drunkard but a master of his craft and another of the few people young Anders had found himself tolerating if not counting among his closest friends, there being very few of those.

When Finn was seated on Angus's back, looking around warily, not certain of his perch but knowing instinctively he was in a better place than he'd been moments ago, Angus swung both animals out into the street and into the roil of clomping horses, rattling wagons, and the din of cursing mule skinners then on out of the wretched town toward the Chama Range humping up cool and blue in the distance, toward the silence and harmony of hearth and home.

Ninety minutes later, Anders Nordic was high in the Chamas among pines and firs, breathing deeply of the gin-scented air under a vaulting sky as blue as his own "startlingly" blue eyes. He swung both horses off the old Indian hunting trail he'd followed off the main trail from town, preferring trails less traveled by others, and into a grove of mixed pines and aspens, midsummer green leaves flashing silver in the late afternoon sunlight.

A creek meandered through the trees, running cool and blue in its shallow bed over pale rocks, murmuring softly, musically. Anders pulled both horses up to the creek, dropped the packhorse's reins, swung down from Apache's back, and dropped the Appaloosa's reins, as well. He'd trained both horses to stay with their ribbons.

With a weary sigh, he slipped the bits from the mouths of both horses so they could draw water freely and loosened their latigos. As he did, the shaggy collie dog leaped down from Angus's back and stood gazing back in the direction from which they'd come, growling deep in his chest, showing his teeth and raising his hackles.

"I know," Anders said, shucking his Winchester '66 from his saddle sheath. He'd traded an Indian pony for the Yellowboy repeater, so named for its brass receiver, five years earlier, laying to rest his old .56 Spencer, though he still used the single-shot rifle for hunting. "Damn fools."

He racked a round into the rifle's breech then walked forward to stand at the top of a rocky rise. Six horseback riders were galloping toward him, the redheaded, little, bowler-hatted banker in the lead atop a fine, black Morgan. Behind him rode yet another beefy man wearing a deputy town marshal star and four others in customary trail gear, all wearing six-guns and holding Winchesters—likely, grub-line riders the banker had pulled out of saloons and hired for a buck or two to comprise his posse of sorts.

Anders had moseyed out of town. He wasn't running from anything or anyone. He'd seen no reason to run and tire his horses. He'd been right, the banker and his vermin urchin as well as the deputy town marshal had been wrong. The banker, however, had quickly gathered men together, including another deputy who looked so much like the one whose face Anders had rearranged, that he must be his brother or at least a cousin. He had the same flat, stupid, belligerent cast to his narrow-eyed gaze. He rode a steeldust gelding just off the left hip of the banker's black.

Seeing Anders standing atop the rocky rise, one foot on a rock before him, holding his repeater down low along his right leg, the little banker raised a gloved hand while pulling back on his reins with the other hand, saying, "Whoa...whoa...whoa! Hold on, you men. Whoa!"

The banker and the other men stared up at Nordic, who gazed back at them blandly. Anders heard thumping sounds behind him and then the collie dog leaped up onto a rock to his right and stood growling at the banker's so-called "posse," hackles raised, tail arched, showing his teeth.

The banker glanced at the dog uncertainly then returned his angry gaze to the big man on the rise before him.

"You can't outrun your crimes, Mr. Nordic. Yes, I learned your name from Mr. McNulty." He glanced at the thickset, sandy-haired man in the battered cream Stetson sitting his steeldust behind him.

The deputy rode up to sit his own horse just off the banker's left stirrup, flaring his nostrils with self-righteous indignation. "You busted my brother's nose, mister. That's assault on a lawman!"

The banker held up his right hand, palm out. "And you damn near busted my wrist!"

"Yeah," added the deputy uncertainly. "You almost busted Mr. English's wrist. And he's a *banker*!"

To English, Anders said, calmly, belying the rage burning inside, "Turn around and ride back to town.

That's where you belong. You keep trailin' me, you're gonna get more than a twisted wrist."

To his right, Finn gave a single, commanding bark.

The banker pointed an angry figure at the collie. "You an' that damn dog are cut from the same cloth, I see!"

"That's why he's here."

"You can't possibly think you're going to get away with what you did in town. *Surely*!"

"Don't call me surely."

"Unruly brigand with a smart mouth to boot!"

Anders scowled, shook his head. "Go home, banker. You don't wanna die here today for that little, nasty, redheaded viper of yours."

"How dare you!"

"Go to hell!"

The banker turned to the deputy, his pasty face red with rage. "Do something, you fool!"

Flushing, the deputy looked at Anders then snapped his rifle up from where it had been resting across his saddle horn. He racked a round into the action and raised it to his shoulder. Anders saw the man's gloved right index finger start to draw back on the trigger. Anders snapped up his own repeater and shot the man out of his saddle. The deputy fired his own repeater wild just before he struck the ground with a resolute thud.

The deputy's horse reared, whinnied shrilly, then wheeled and galloped back in the direction from which it had come, reins bouncing along the ground beside it.

Anders's bullet had taken the man in his chest.

He lay unmoving in the grass and sage.

To Anders's right, Finn barked once as though in satisfaction. The dog probably had history with the deputy—another mindless thug.

The others stared down at him in hang-jawed shock.

Anders recocked the '66 and kept it aimed at the men before him. To the banker he said, "Now, look what you've done."

The banker narrowed his little, mean eyes at him as he pointed down at the deputy. "You killed that man in cold blood!"

"Nothin' cold-blooded about it. Just practical."

"You sure are fast for a big man!" accused one of the others whom English had probably found in a saloon and was in need of more drinking and poker money. His eyes were bright from popskull.

"When you stand out in a crowd," Anders said, "it pays to be good with a fire-stick."

The others flanking the banker looked at each other. Then the man who'd just spoken reined his horse around sharply and put the spurs to it, galloping back the way they'd all come, his saddlebags flapping like wings against his horse's hips. To a man, the others except the banker followed suit.

"Wait!" English cried. "Hold on! Get back here. I paid you all in advance. This man *shall* be arrested for murder"—he turned to Anders scowling angrily and with deep frustration—"and for threatening a child with bodily harm."

"I threaten you with bodily harm, mister. If I ever

see your face again, I'm gonna pump one through your forehead. Now, get the hell out of here before my wolf breaks loose and I do it now and save havin' to do it later!"

Finn showed his teeth at the banker, growling.

The banker flinched as though he'd been slapped. He gazed fearfully down at the big man who was obviously as good with a rifle as he was with his fists. Gritting his teeth, he reined his Morgan around, yelled, "Hi-*yaahh!*" and galloped back after the others.

"This is not over!" he yelled behind him.

Anders scowled his dismay. "No," he said to himself. "It never is."

CHAPTER THREE

An hour later, with the light dying fast as the sun sank behind the high, western ridges that stood in sharp, black silhouette against its painter's pallet of ochres, greens, reds, and salmons, Anders rode into the headquarters of the ranch he currently rode for, so to speak. The line shack was another two thousand feet higher than the Flying W headquarters' eight thousand feet, on a ridge that stood like a giant blacksmith's anvil to the south, gauzy with the soft blue-green of pine, fir, and spruce forest, and which he was so eager to reach he'd nearly bypassed the headquarters and headed straight for it.

He was hungry and he yearned for the silent tranquility of cooking his supper alone in his cabin, under a lens-clear sky of candle-like starlight. Alone, that was, save for his new friend, Finn, who'd taken to him even faster than had most of the other animals in his life. What Anders Nordic lacked in his relations with both children and adults of the human species, he more than made up for in his relations with animals.

Especially the disenfranchised kind.

He'd rather be heading straight for his cabin, but he owed it to his boss to warn her of the trouble he'd likely brought to the Flying W.

As he rode up to the long, low, L-shaped cabin in the dying light, he saw the silhouette of his female boss clad in a loose wool work shirt and tight denims splitting wood to the cabin's right, a nice-sized pile growing near the chopping block. Miss Maggie Rae, widow of Magnus Tobias Rae, to whom she'd been married for twenty-six years before he'd been killed by a mountain lion, having ridden out alone to check his herd one crisp autumn evening, just then raised the maul high over her head and with a mannish grunt thrust it down and expertly through the pine log perched on the chopping block, cleaving it cleanly in three separate stove-sized chunks.

In the corner of her right eye, she must have seen the big man's approach with his two horses and the dog riding a little more certainly than when they'd first left town. Leaving the maul in the block, the tough, spidery little woman, craggy-faced and skinny and with not a single strand of gray in the black hair she wore pulled back and knotted tightly at the top of her head, puffed the quirley dangling out one corner of her mouth. She took the cigarette between the thumb and index finger of her right hand, tapped off the ash with her middle finger, and said, "Well, well, well…look what the cat dragged in. My own rogue griz come acallin'!" She glanced at the cabin behind her, the windows lit against the coming night. "Clara, break out the china—we got company!"

Maggie Rae wheezed a laugh seasoned by years of smoking and sipping her own homemade wine that was stronger than some corn mash Anders had sampled. To Anders's left, the cabin's front door opened and Maggie Rae's niece, Clara, walked out onto the small stoop, a black cat perched on one shoulder. She moved to the rail and stood there, staring toward the big man on the Appaloosa, absently patting the big cat on her shoulder and which appeared half asleep.

"It's Anders," she said, as though to herself.

"What brings ya?" Maggie asked him. "I've never known you to be the sociable sort."

Holding his reins taut in his left hand, as was his habit, leaving the right one free for the Colt on his right thigh, Anders said, "I been to town. Supply run. Think I mighta brought trouble."

"Mighta?"

"I brought trouble."

"What kind?"

"There's a deputy town marshal laid out along Crow Creek, where the Flying W graze starts."

"Hmm." Maggie Rae nodded slowly, grimly. "What happened?"

Anders sighed. "There was a kid teasin' a dog with a stick. This dog." He tossed his head back to indicate Finn on the packhorse. "I threatened the kid. His father objected, brought a deputy. The deputy ended up with a broken beak."

"Ha!" Maggie Rae cackled, throwing her head back and slapping her thigh with her left hand. "I knew *that* was comin'!" She took a quick puff off the quirley, making the coal glow briefly, then blew the smoke plume toward the first kindling stars.

"The kid was the banker's son."

Maggie Rae cackled even louder. "I knew *that* was comin', too!"

"How?"

"You might keep to yourself, but I know you well enough to know you wouldn't threaten a pauper's son."

Anders winced.

"Thought I'd better let you know. I'll clear out, if you want."

He didn't want to clear out. You couldn't run from trouble. If it wasn't faced head on, resolved, trouble had a way of dogging a man's heels. But Anders didn't like to involve others in his. Maggie Rae had only three other men working for her. They were likely currently enjoying a quiet supper of elk steaks and coffee laced with popskull in the small, window-lit, log bunkhouse on the other side of the yard from the main lodge. All three were old and they mostly used their guns merely to hammer coffee beans around branding or roundup fires.

They'd be no good against trouble. Oh, they'd hang a rustler now and then and scare away nesters, but they'd be no good against real trouble. Town trouble.

"I need that line shack occupied till the fall gather," said Maggie Rae, walking slowly toward Anders, taking another puff off the quirley that was no longer than her skinny, Indian-brown right finger down to the first knuckle. "You're the one I want to occupy it. Rustlers and nesters steer clear of you, and so will Bryce Adams, if he knows what's good fer him." She nodded her certainty, pursing her lips. "He's the only man with half a brain in Cimarron. He'll ride out here soon enough. We'll have a sit-down chat over my chokecherry wine." She smiled cunningly. "He'll ride back to town with a big ol' grin on his face. He always does."

She winked.

"If you say so, ma'am," Anders said with a sigh.

She looked at Finn sitting on Angus's back just like he'd been born to the packsaddle. "That's the dog, eh?"

"Yeah."

Finn showed his teeth at her but did not growl.

Maggie chuckled. "Looks like he's got the bark on."

"He's cautious of others, as others haven't been too good to him."

"But then, he probably hasn't been good to too many others, either."

"Good point."

Maggie turned back to Anders and smiled knowingly, then nodded. "Best get on home. Dark soon."

She glanced back at her niece, Clara Vaughn, still standing on the porch, staring this way. "I know she wants me to invite you to supper, but I know you won't stay."

Anders glanced at the young woman on the porch. Not so young, really. She was twenty-seven but she had a strange, earthy remoteness about her, an innocence of one half her age. She'd never married. Her family had died in a milk fever on a little ranch around Mesilla. Her mother had been Mexican, her father Norski, like Anders. She'd been orphaned at sixteen, and the men in and around Mesilla had not treated her well. Maggie, who'd been widowed around that time, had ridden down to Mesilla and brought her back here to the Flying W, where she's lived ever since.

Understandably, she never went to town. Never, as far as Anders knew, associated with anyone but her cat and her aunt.

She spoke with an odd, beguiling accent, a mix of Norwegian and Spanish, betraying her mixed heritage. Her eyes and hair betrayed it, too—dark brown hair, gray-green eyes. A pretty woman. Downright haunting.

Anders didn't like her. Or, more to the point, he didn't like how he felt when he was around her. He was glad it was dark enough that he couldn't see her clearly. Still, her silent gaze was strangely hypnotizing, affecting.

Anders looked away from her.

"Well, then," he said, pinching his hat brim to Maggie Rae.

"You'll be left alone," Maggie told him as he reined Apache and Angus around, Finn keeping his cautious gaze on the lady rancher. "I'll see to it. Won't be hard. The only people who know about that line shack are the men who lived in it over the years, and most of them are dead."

Laughing deep in her chest, making an odd wheezing sound, shoulders jerking, the owner and operator of the Flying W drew deep on the quirley and, blowing out the smoke, flicked the stub into the yard which sparked as it hit the ground and bounced.

———

Cimarron town marshal Bryce Adams rode into town about the same time.

Anders Nordic was heading back to the sanctuary of his line shack. Adams was looking forward to the sanctuary of his small, neat house just around the corner from his office which had two strap-iron cages along the back wall and four more cages in the stone basement. The building was brick and solid, and it needed to be. While Adams wasn't housing any prisoners at the moment, on weekends it filled up fast. Cimarron was growing, and so was the crime rate, though at the moment it consisted mainly of drunk miners and punchers stomping with their tails up.

Adams and his two deputies, Lon and Dave Dempsey, managed to keep the lid on, though Adams often wished his help was a little better seasoned and not quite as hotheaded as both brothers were. In these remote reaches, however, a head lawman had to play the cards he was dealt.

He wanted to go right home, but he'd been gone all day, delivering a prisoner to Socorro, and he'd better check in with one or both of the Dempsey brothers, though one, if he was doing his job correctly, as Adams was always instructing them to do, should be out making the rounds, twisting doorknobs of the locked businesses and strolling through the town's half dozen saloons.

Keeping the peace.

A saddled horse was tied at the hitchrack. That would be Lon's. There was also a leather, red-wheeled carriage parked in front of the building. Adams knew the fancy rig belonged to the town's sole banker, Reginald English, an uppity little popinjay with a temper to boot.

Adams groaned. *Something happened when I was away. I shouldn't be surprised. It usually does.* Adams had a feeling someone had tried or accomplished a holdup at English's Stockman's Bank of Cimarron.

Great.

That meant more riding as well as tracking tomorrow, and Adams's forty-year-old behind was raw from today's trek. Used to be he could ride all day, hazing herds from the Brazos River country to the railheads in Kansas and then be ready to stomp with his tail up with his trail pards all night. Those days were over. They'd been over the past fifteen years.

He swung down from his dapple gray's back and tossed the reins over the hitchrack, beside Lon's brown-and-white pinto. He hitched his pants up on his hips, wincing at the burn in his backside as well as the wind- and sunburn on his cheeks, and heavily climbed the three steps to the jailhouse's front stoop. He'd taken one step toward the door when the door suddenly opened, and the dapper, little, redheaded banker stood scowling up at him.

"What have you been up to all day, Marshal? We've been waiting for you for over an hour!"

Adams pushed past the little man, walking into his office. He removed his hat and was about to peg it on the wall by the door when he saw Lon Dempsey leaning leisurely back in his chair behind Adams's rolltop desk. The man's nose, twice its normal size, wore a thick white bandage. The man's cheeks and eyes were purple. No, the eyes were *black*. Both were swollen to slits.

Adams couldn't help but give a chuckle. "What happened to you?" He and his brother were always running off at the mouth and getting themselves beat up in one of the saloons or brothels.

The little banker closed the office door and walked around to stand scowling up at the taller Adams, the little man's freckled cheeks crimson above the mustache he must have paid a whole dollar weekly to have trimmed. That would have to be a good half-morning job.

"A big bear of a Dakota lunatic named Anders Nordic is what happened to him, Marshal." The banker pointed at the deputy, the gold ring on his pinky flashed in the lantern light. "And his brother lay dead along Crow Creek on Mrs. Rae's Flying W range!"

"Dead?"

"That's what they tell me," Lon Dempsey said. He sat back in the chair like it was his, hands entwined on his belly.

"And you're leaving him there?" Adams said, trying to restrain his anger.

"What can I do?" said the deputy, indignant. "It hurts to move. Hell, it hurts to breathe. Lookin' at you, I see two of you!"

"Yeah, well, I admit one's enough," the lawman dryly quipped. Holding his hat in his hands, he hiked a hip on the desk abutting the wall to his right and at which his deputies did their paperwork and ate their lunches. "What happened? Start from the beginning."

"You're not going to like it, Marshal," the banker said. "But, by God, something needs to be done!"

"Oh, I already don't like it," Adams said with a fateful sigh.

He had a very strong feeling his life was about to get a whole lot more complicated.

CHAPTER FOUR

I t was good and dark, stars stretching across the large, black, bowl-shaped sky so thickly they resembled flour smeared across black velvet, when Anders reached his cabin that crouched just beyond a bench at the base of a forested ridge—as concealed as a hermit's hovel.

The weary wayfarer crossed the shallow, unnamed stream fronting the bench, then climbed up and over the bench to the shack hunched in the darkness below the rise and off-loaded his recently acquired stores on the cabin's small front stoop. He secured the horses in the stable and corral that flanked the cabin off its left rear corner.

Finn watched him, sitting a ways out from the stable's open doors, keeping a cautious eye on the restive night around the cabin and stable, ears pricked, tail curled around him. He jerked his head this way and that, sniffing, growling, likely smelling wolves, possibly night stalking wildcats.

New country for Finn. A dog like the collie, half-wild, mistreated, would be on guard for all possible threats. Anders knew something about that himself, for he was the same way whenever he found himself in a new place, spending the first few nights scouting around with his rifle and sleeping with his pistol under his saddle.

When he'd rubbed each horse down thoroughly, and had fed and watered them, he turned them out into the corral and closed the stable doors.

"Come on, boy," he told Finn, heading around the cabin toward the front. "Let's fix us a meal. I feel as empty as a dead man's boot."

The dog followed slowly, hesitantly, head down, mewling deep in his throat. Just because the man had thrown him a bone did not mean the man had gained his complete trust. That was a prize to be won slowly, gradually over time.

Anders unlocked the padlock on the cabin door, opened the door, kicked a rock in place to prop it open, and went inside and fumbled around in the darkness to light the lamp hanging over the kitchen table by a rusty wire. Anders turned up the wick. In the watery light, the cabin came to life—crudely furnished but homey, the sitting area to the left, a cot abutting the rear wall and covered with a thick bearskin against the ubiquitous mountain chill.

The kitchen area lay to the right with cupboards, dry sink, squat black range, and eating table near the sashed window in the front wall. There were rugs on the floor, a few skins tacked to the walls as well as a watercolor of a waterfall in a beaver meadow and which Anders assumed one of the cabin's previous dwellers had painted to help fill the long, quiet nights.

Anders put his stores away in his slow, purposeful, deliberate way, filling shelves and cupboards with canned and dry goods including coffee and buckwheat for pancakes. In the cellar beneath a trapdoor in the kitchen floor, he stored cream, two large wheels of cheese, two dozen fresh eggs, a bag of potatoes and one of onions, several flitches of bacon and two sausages large as howitzer shells.

Those were what Anders considered luxury items. When they ran out in two weeks or so, he'd survive on what comprised the bulk of his diet—wild berries, roots, onions, mushrooms, and the meat of rabbits, deer, and elk he trapped or shot in the forest above the cabin and stored in the keeper shed behind the stable.

When he'd filled his larder, so to speak, he walked out onto the stoop.

Finn sat a way out from the cabin, lying belly down, paws crossed, still looking around suspiciously.

"We'll eat soon, boy. You can come in if you want. It's up to you."

The dog turned to him. Anders heard Finn growl very quietly, an automatic response. The dog was sensitized to threat. It would take a good, long time for him to let his guard down. He'd never completely let it down, not after the kind of life he'd led up to now. Anders figured he was still young, maybe two or three —but he'd come to trust Anders eventually, come to feel at home here just as Anders had...eventually.

With the split wood from the bin beside the range, he built a fire and set water for coffee to boil. While the range ticked and groaned as it heated, and the coffeepot began to sound like a breeze in the pine crowns, he pulled a chair out from the table, positioned it before the range, and slacked into it heavily. He'd smoke a cigarette and drink a cup of coffee before he made his meal. He needed a breather. Long day.

He pulled his makins sack out from under his tunic, where it hung from a braided leather thong around his neck, produced a rolling paper which he troughed between two fingers, and dribbled the newly purchased chopped Durham onto it and, licking one edge, adeptly rolled it closed until he had a nice, tight cylinder to which he touched the flames of a match he'd scratched to life on his thumbnail.

When the water boiled, he dumped a fistful of the fresh coffee into it, let it come to a boil again, removed it from the range to the table, and settled the grounds with a little fresh, cold water he hauled from the creek every morning and kept in a clay pot on the porch.

He sank back in the chair, steaming tin coffee cup in one hand, smoldering quirley in the other.

Long day.

A day with repercussions, most likely.

Should never go to town. Should always rely on his foraging and hunting skills for his stores. That's all he needed, really. Somewhere along the line, he'd gone soft. He'd found himself depending on town for luxury items.

Foolish.

Now he'd killed a deputy town marshal, and men would be hunting him.

Leastways, if the banker had his way.

But Anders had had no choice but to shoot the deputy. The man would have shot him. He'd had to shoot him because Anders was not going to let him arrest him. The only thing he dreaded worse than an iron cell was to be buried alive, both of which he often had nightmares about.

He should pull out. Spare himself and Maggie Rae the trouble.

Damnable pride would keep him here, likely lead to more killing. He would not run. He'd done nothing wrong but stop a kid from tormenting a dog then defending himself against false imprisonment. Maggie had said they wouldn't find him here. But if they wanted to badly enough, they'd keep scouring the mountains until they did.

And they'd die for their stupidity.

Anders Nordic was one man you didn't back into a corner.

But they didn't know that. No one knew him well enough to know that. He'd lived alone for too long for anyone to get to know him. And that's how he'd wanted it. The only men who'd gotten to know him too well were dead.

He finished his coffee, stubbed out his cigarette, then chucked more wood into the stove and set about making his supper—beans, which he'd soaked in a pot throughout the day, with bacon and a pan of cornbread, which he washed down with the coffee. He fried Finn a pan of bacon and set it out in front of the stoop. The dog lay where he'd been before. Now he thumped his tail and came running to quickly gobble up every bit of bacon and to lick the pan clean afterward.

Then he returned to his previous place in the yard, once again on guard.

Anders went back inside, heated water, and used it to clean his dishes in the dry sink. When he'd swabbed off the table and returned all the pans and other utensils to their rightful places, he opened the trap door and fished one of his last ales up from the cellar. He opened the lock, poured the rich, dark ale into a heavy stone mug, the thick froth like that on the shore of a cold river, the beer itself smelling like chocolate and oats, and went out onto the stoop to drink it in the hide-bottom chair he kept to the right of the door.

The night couldn't be quieter. Occasionally a lone coyote would yammer from a ridge. Others would join in and the bizarre choir would continue for a minute or so, maybe answered by another one from a different direction, and then silence would reign once more. Finn didn't react to the coyotes. He'd been on his own in the high desert outside Cimarron to know coyotes and to not be afraid. He likely knew most of the wild animals. The one he was most wary of was man.

Anders had enjoyed half his beer, boots crossed on the railing before him, rocked back in his chair, when Finn suddenly turned his head to stare down the slope and across the creek into the forest beyond. His ears stood straight up, and he worked his nose, sniffing.

Anders dropped his feet to the porch floor and straightened in the chair, frowning. "What is it, boy?"

Finn kept staring intently, listening for a full minute, before Anders heard a growl rumble up from deep in the dog's chest. Finn rose suddenly, continued staring, tail arched, then suddenly started barking. All at once, he took off running down the grade, across the creek and into the forest beyond, barking wildly.

"Uff da," Anders said, raking a big paw down his face in consternation. "He's mighty riled."

The wild barking continued, echoing across the quiet night and dwindling toward the glittering stars, for several more seconds before stopping abruptly.

Just like that, the barking stopped.

Once more, silence deepened around the cabin.

Standing now, staring over the bench and across the stream, Anders's heart beat heavily, worriedly, as he wondered what had caused the dog to stop barking so abruptly. Then a horseback rider emerged from the woods on the other side of the creek. Riding slowly, the man put his horse across the stream, the water splashing silver around the horse's hocks in the starlight, and then disappeared as he started up the slope toward the cabin.

Apprehension causing the short hairs to prickle along the back of Anders's neck, the big Dakotan rose from his chair, making it creak, and reached into his cabin for his Winchester, which he'd leaned against the door frame, fully loaded and ready. Now as he turned to face the slope, he slowly, quietly levered a round into the rifle's action and held it one-handed up high across his chest, hooking his right thumb behind his shell belt, near the long-barreled Colt .44 hanging low on his right thigh.

He wasn't wearing his hat, and a vagrant night breeze tussled his blond hair that curled over his ears and hung down over his collar.

Hoof thuds rose, gradually growing louder.

Then the rider appeared—the man's hat first then his face obscured by the darkness. The man rode a bay horse with one front white sock. He continued toward the cabin, riding slowly, the horse plodding along, a glitter in its eye, wanting to run but the rider held its reins taut in his right hand. As horse and rider grew larger before him, Anders saw the "man's" curved, supple figure, their chest too lumpy for a man behind the light tan canvas coat she wore.

Anders slackened his hold on the Winchester's neck and lowered the rifle to hang straight down along his right leg and said at the end of a long sigh, "Clara."

The young woman reined the bay up close to the porch and leaned forward, resting one arm on her saddle horn. She wore gloves and tight denims, and her long, dark brown hair was touched by the night breeze, several locks blown back behind her cheeks, revealing her heart-shaped face with full lips and broad cheekbones.

"Sounds like you got yourself in a pack of trouble, mister. My aunt's worried."

"What're you doing here?"

"I got restless." She stared at him flatly, though there was a vaguely taunting, amused cast to her gaze.

"You shouldn't have come. You might have been followed."

She grinned shrewdly, making her smooth, tanned cheeks dimple. In her odd accent, she said, "I don't do that."

"Just the same…like you said. I got trouble."

She stared at him in her singular silence.

She'd been to the cabin before. The first few times she'd just skulked around on horseback, watching him, staying about seventy yards out away from the shack. Then one day while he'd been repairing a bridle inside at his kitchen table, she'd ridden up and asked for a cup of coffee. She'd tied her horse at the rack fronting the cabin and come in and sipped her coffee at the table, watching him oddly, scowling, but didn't say anything.

She'd simply finished her coffee, untied her horse, mounted up, and loped off down the slope, across the stream, and into the forested rise beyond.

Later, she'd shown up one morning for breakfast. She'd said she'd forgotten to pack bacon. She'd been out hunting. The day before she'd shot a young doe. It was slumped across her packhorse. Apparently, she'd camped in the mountains alone—Nordic had the feeling she did that quite a bit. He fed her breakfast and they'd talked and even laughed a little before she'd gathered the dishes, washed them, put them away, then left again without another word, just galloped over the bench, down the slope, across the stream, and into the woods.

Now Anders scowled at her curiously. "What'd you do to my dog?"

Suddenly, she smiled. Anders was surprised. He'd never really seen her smile, but only scowl as though to hide whatever thoughts were roiling around behind her pretty hazel eyes. "Gave him a bone." Her smile broadened, turned crooked so that she was smiling with more of the left side of her mouth than the right side. "Big ol' beef bone, plenty of meat left on it, full o' marrow."

"Why, that's downright sneaky."

"That's me." She swung fleetly down from the bay's saddle. "Sneaky." She looked at the beer bottle on the porch rail. "Got one o' them for me?"

CHAPTER FIVE

The next morning, Cimarron Town Marshal Bryce Adams woke with a splitting headache.

When he opened his eyes, the pearl wash of dawn light pushing through the lace curtains over the window felt like several miniature javelins piercing his eyes.

"Oh," he said, gritting his teeth and placing his left hand over his forehead, digging his fingers in as though to drive the misery away.

The bed moved as Angela rolled over to face him, her curly, flaxen hair like a tumbleweed around her head. Strands of it hung down to obscure her face, which appeared particularly soft and pale and youthful in the mornings—if not so much as the day drew on—reminding him again, nettlingly, of how much younger she was than he. She was twenty-three, he was forty, and with each day that passed, he felt every year of it a little more.

"I told you," she said, snuggling up close against

him. "That busthead you get at the Who Hit John is gonna kill you one day."

Adams groaned, massaged his aching temples. The pain seemed to be originating behind his right eye and fanning out from there, every breath he took causing it to fan out from its source like ripples on an otherwise still lake.

"Don't know what it is about that stuff," he said, pushing himself up to a sitting position. "But while it burns going down it seems to take the edge off a man's troubles."

"But you pay for it, don't you, honey?"

"Yes, I do."

Adams tossed his covers back and swung his feet to the floor and sat there at the edge of the bed, waiting for the pain to abate. It likely wouldn't till noon. He was afraid that if he got up too quickly, he might pass out. Angela was right. He needed to stay out of the Who Hit John. He found himself patronizing the place, sitting alone at a table in the shadows of a rear corner when his life or his job bubbled up with one particularly vexing problem or another.

Now that problem was the banker, Reginald English and likely the father of his dearly departed deputy. Aidan Dempsey's Crosshatch spread abutted Maggie Rae's Flying W.

Adams didn't know if the rancher had heard the grim news of his son's death, but when he did, he'd grow a pair of horns that would likely put the banker's to shame. The men were business partners and now they both had something else in common—a rage sharply focused on the big Dakota loner, Anders Nordic, whom most referred to as "the Nordic." He was new to this area and lived in a remote line shack on the Flying W Ranch. He'd gotten crossways with English when he'd given his boy hell for tormenting a dog and then did not show the banker the respect English thought he deserved.

Had, in fact, made a laughingstock out of the mean little banker in the Who Hit John and made a fool out of Lon Dempsey when Nordic had turned the deputy's nose sideways.

Adams doubted his two deputies' father, Aidan Dempsey, one of the largest, wealthiest, and most respected stockmen in the county, felt any real love for his "boys," which was what he called them despite Dave having been twenty-six and Lon being two years older. But they were the man's family, by God, and when you messed with a Dempsey—he had two sons and a daughter—you messed with their powerful father and his hired men.

Aidan had sent his sons to town because neither was worth a damn on the ranch and he wanted them to carve positions of power for themselves in the county, one eventually taking over Adams's job and the other running for public office. Adams had learned this secondhand from a friend on the town council. Dave had been reading nights with an attorney here in town, intending eventually to set up his own practice, an odious notion to Adams. He and most everyone else in the area knew Dave Dempsey was as dumb as a boot. The son's father either didn't see it or didn't want to see it. Aidan Dempsey was a man who yearned for control in political matters, and what better way to have that control than to have sons in positions of political power?

Even though they weren't cut from the right cloth for it.

Hell, they weren't much good as deputies, either. If they wielded any respect at all it was due to their names, not because of their prowess or fearlessness as lawmen. Adams had taken them on because, their father being who he was, and in league with English, Adams didn't have much choice. Also, he didn't have many options. The positions paid only a few dollars a month more than did cowpunching jobs, and in most cowpunching jobs you didn't have to worry about having a whiskey bottle broken over your head or getting drilled in the back with a .45 by a drunk gambler with a chip on his shoulder.

Adams inhaled deeply, steeling himself against the pain in his head, and heaved himself up off the bed to his feet.

"Ah, Jesus!" he complained, stumbling forward, reaching for his socks thrown over a chair with the rest of his attire.

"Why don't you spend the morning in bed, hon?" Angela said, rummaging in a drawer of her bedside table. "I'll make you some eggs later. I don't have to go in until six tonight. We can have all day."

"Can't," Adams said, stumbling around as he tried pulling his right sock on. Finally, he gave up and sat down on the bed to pull it on. "There was trouble yesterday when I was away. Here in town. Then…in the mountains."

"What kind of trouble, hon?"

Adams glanced over his shoulder at Angela, whom he'd married only a year ago despite their age difference…and whose father was another rich man—a wealthy mine owner named Fitzsimmons who didn't approve of Adams any more than he did his daughter. To say that Angela had a troubled past, including a failed marriage, was putting it mildly. Still, the man, who owned a large house on the edge of town, was a thorn in Adams's side, forcing money on him so that the town's unwealthy, unworthy lawman, could give his daughter the semblance of a decent life.

The damnable thing of it was, Adams took it despite how wretched he felt taking the man's money to support his daughter, who danced in the local Opera House—a fancy name for a glorified hurdy-gurdy house—and was an embarrassment to both Fitzsimmons and his wife, both of whom brushed elbows and oiled the palms of territorial congressmen in Albuquerque.

Angela was just then taking several pulls from the small, flat, blue bottle garishly labeled *Dr. Lermontov's Snake Oil Elixir*, which Adams knew was really nothing more than laudanum—a pinch of peppermint, gunpowder, and likely a few tablespoons of actual snake venom. She bought it from a Russian con artist named Lermontov who called himself a doctor, though he was really just a swindler in a threadbare, checked suit and ragged bowler hat, who rolled through town once a month in his gaudy covered wagon and delivered his "medicine," which Angela claimed she needed for her back injured in a fall while dancing three years ago, to Adams's back door.

When Bryce wasn't home, of course. If he'd ever caught the man delivering that poison, he'd have shot him.

"Angela, why are you drinking that crap?"

She pulled the bottle down and gave him her snooty look. "Same reason you drink the busthead at the Who Hit John, Bryce." She took another pull, insolently smacked her lips, then returned the bottle to its drawer.

"The busthead at the John is probably better than that slop is for you. Besides, I know how much you pay for it."

"Don't worry," Angela said, lifting her chin with a sneer and tossing her hair back from her cheeks. "I have my own money but even if I didn't, we both know you could afford it."

That stung Adams worse than the little man in his head smashing a big hammer against his brain plate. Bryce knew Angela must have known about her father's handouts, but she'd never mentioned it before until now.

Adams, fuming, his pride in the gutter, had no response. He just finished dressing, drew on his boots, buckled his gun and shell belt around his waist, and donned his denim jacket and low-crowned brown Stetson on his way out the back door. He had no appetite even for coffee. He saddled his horse in the stable behind the house, and it was a sullen, aching, and defeated town lawman who rode out of the yard and along Cimarron's backstreets still obscured with early shadows to the main drag and his small, log office and jailhouse.

The office door was still padlocked, which was how he'd left it the night before. Which meant Lon Dempsey either wasn't in yet or would take the day off to nurse his broken beak. At the moment, Adams didn't care. His day's task of fetching his deputy's dead brother back to Cimarron occupied the brunt of his aching brain. He wanted to fetch it before Aidan Dempsey got wind of it and rode into the mountains to bring the body back himself then go on a long, Dempsey-like tear of vengeance that might very well touch a flame to a dynamite fuse.

It had happened before.

This very thing was how range wars got started.

The mountains were under Adams's jurisdiction just because the town council had deemed it so, as there was no near sheriff, and rustlers were a constant problem on the ranges up in those remote reaches.

Adams sat his dapple gray, gazing toward the Chama Range rising in silhouette against the growing wash of gray in the east. A strange, ominous feeling grew in him, beneath the pounding of the injurious pulse in his tender head. He'd seen the Nordic only once or twice before, on one of the man's rare trips to town for supplies. He'd been living in a line shack on Mrs. Rae's land since early spring, so roughly four months. Adams knew roughly where one of the line shacks lay but not the other two.

He knew that Mrs. Rae's husband, Magnus Rae, had built three cabins in the remote stretches of the Chamas, living in them as a mountain man who hunted and trapped before he married Maggie, the daughter of an itinerant preacher, homesteaded a parcel, and gradually built and grew the Flying W. His ranch had never been large by Chama standards, but he'd run several hundred cattle on government graze, butting heads with one or two ranchers once or twice and, though his payroll had always been small, had managed to keep his graze free of nesters, free-grazers, and rustlers, whom he hung on sight just as the rest of the Chama ranchers did.

He'd usually kept at least one cabin occupied from spring to fall. They were well hidden, hard to find. Magnus had built them when the Indians still had the run of this country, and he'd purposefully made them damn near invisible. As hard to find as a well-hidden mine.

Adams thought that the Nordic was likely holed up in one of those cabins. That was why Adams had decided that, after he'd collected Dave Dempsey's body, he'd ride to the Flying W headquarters and have a palaver with Mrs. Rae.

Time to do that now.

He booted the gray gelding into a fast walk down the thickly shadowed main drag that was still waking up, shopkeepers sweeping their walks or setting out displays, a few horsebackers leaving gambling dens and parlor houses to climb heavily into their saddles. A long ranch-supply wagon rattled into town from the south and Adams pinched his hat brim to old Mordecai Green, the former cowpuncher and current cook out on the Triple Circle 9 not far from town. The graybeard gave a slow, acknowledging dip of his chin as he passed, chewing a fat cigar stub, the empty supply wagon barking over chuckholes.

When the shacks and cabins outlying Cimarron fell back behind the lawman, he reached back and fished a bottle out of a saddlebag pouch. He pried out the cork with his teeth and, muttering, "Li'l hair o' the dog," took two deep pulls of the same previous night's whiskey that had spawned the little man with the big hammer in his head. He returned the cork to the bottle and returned it to the pouch.

Adams ran the sleeve of his jacket across his mouth. "That helps," he said, buoyed by an abatement of the throbbing pain in his skull. "I'll be damned if that don't help…"

He chuckled, belying his mental self-flagellation for his long, slow tumble from a former propriety…

He swung the gelding, Cimarron, onto a two-track secondary trail and a nettling dread building inside him at what he would find on Flying W graze, his own deputy killed by the strange loner from Dakota, started the slow, gradual climb through stony dikes and shelving mesas and into a canyon that would lead him into the Chama's higher reaches, into the yawning, dark fate that awaited him.

Eventually, the trail joined up with Crow Creek,

twisting and turning through aspens, cedars, pines, and firs. As he climbed still higher, deep blue, short-needled spruces pushed up along the trail on Adams's left and on the creek's opposite bank on his right, the forest and high, rocky ridges around him keeping the canyon in perpetual dawn.

Warm, buttery sunlight washed over him as he reached the top of the pass and then swung right when he saw the deep horseshoe bend in the cut of the creek, which was the area that the banker, Reginald English, had described as the spot the Nordic had shot Dave Dempsey out of his saddle. Adams didn't have trouble finding the body, for turkey buzzards had found it, as well. They were swarming over it, leaping and quarreling and spreading their massive wings. Adams hazed them off without firing his pistol. He didn't want to announce his presence here. He didn't yet want the mountain people to know what had happened, though surely the word would spread—was probably spreading right now, in fact—before he could figure out what to do about it.

As he retrieved Dave's horse, which was idly grazing roughly fifty yards from the body, and wrapped the body in Dave's own soogan, he went over what he intended to do about the situation in his mind. The long ride from town had given him plenty of time.

It was with a sense of building dread that, once he had Dave Dempsey's blanket-wrapped body lying belly down across his saddle, he booted the gray, trailing Dave's lineback dun by its bridle reins, in the direction of Mrs. Rae's Flying W.

CHAPTER SIX

"Well, look what the cat dragged in!" bellowed Maggie Rae forty-five minutes later, as Adams rode into the headquarters of the Flying W and reined up in front of the lodge.

Mrs. Rae had just stepped out the lodge's front door and onto the stoop, loudly cocking the old Henry repeating rifle in her spidery, brown hands. The sleeves of her men's dark blue work shirt were rolled to her elbows, and the cuffs of her men's dark blue denims were rolled up to her ankles, revealing the men's moccasin-soft stockman's boots she wore.

Adams couldn't remember her ever dressing any other way, even when she was twenty years younger.

He thumbed his Stetson up on his forehead and gave a cockeyed smile. "Good afternoon, Mrs. Rae." He wasn't sure if it was morning or noon. Judging by the sun kiting nearly straight up, and the shortness of the shadows, it was nearly noon or just after.

"'Mrs. Rae,' is it, Bryce? This must be serious."

Her voice was typically nasal. It sounded like a saw cutting through oak. She canted her head to study Dave Dempsey's horse flanking Adams's gray. "Who you got there? Better not be one of my men!"

"One of mine," Adams said.

"Ah."

"I guess you probably knew that, didn't you, Maggie?"

Maggie didn't say anything. She stood atop the porch steps, holding the rifle up high across her bird-like chest.

"Could do with a cup of coffee," Adams said when the woman didn't make the invitation, which she usually did when the lawman stopped at the Flying W while out hunting rustlers or owlhoots cooling their heels in the mountains.

Maggie gazed at him critically for a few more stretched seconds then lowered the Winchester. "*Mi casa, tu casa*. You know that, Bryce."

She turned and walked through the cabin's open door.

Adams swung down from Cimarron's back, tied both the dapple gray and the lineback dun to the hitchrack fronting the cabin. He climbed the steps, crossed the porch, and stepped through the open doorway. He removed his hat and stood just inside as Maggie Rae filled two stone mugs with steaming black coffee at the long table to the lawman's left and abutted by a wooden bench on each side. This was the kitchen half of the roomy, rustically furnished cabin—skins and game trophies on every wall and a large bearskin on the floor fronting the big fieldstone hearth at the other end of the lodge, to Adams's right.

The lawman smiled. He remembered Magnus riding back to the ranch one early winter with the heavy skin rolled onto the back of a packhorse, a travois carrying the meat. He'd been drunk as a lord and happy as a man who'd just discovered a cache of hidden gold.

The old rancher had loved to hunt, which recalled for him his simpler, more adventurous younger years living and hunting and trapping in the mountains surrounding what was now his and Maggie's ranch.

"You're looking a little green around the gills, Bryce," Maggie said when they were seated across from each other, a mug steaming on the table before them. "Long night?"

They'd been on a first-name basis for years. Adams had once worked for Maggie and Magnus, back when he was young and as wild as a two-year-old bronc. For three years, he'd ridden the range and broken horses for the Raes, and he still had a gimpy hip to show for it. He didn't limp but that bruised bone always informed him in no uncertain terms when a storm was on the way.

Adams lifted the mug to his lips, blew ripples on the coal black mud, and sipped. Swallowing, setting the mug back down, he sighed and ran a hand through his short, sandy hair that showed more than a few strands of gray at the temples as well as in his dragoon-style mustache. "You could say that." He looked across the table at her, pointedly. "Don't tell me you don't know why I'm here, Maggie."

The woman—whose age Adams had never known though she'd always looked around fifty, even twenty years ago when Adams had first taken the job here to oblige his father who had tried desperately to keep his wild boy from going outlaw, as several of his friends had—shook her head. "Nope. Wouldn't do that, Bryce. For old times' sake, if nothin' else. You were a good hand." She smiled suddenly, causing the deep lines webbing her face to carve deeper into her Indian-dark skin. "After Magnus had worked the green off'n you, leastways."

"I'll always be honest with you."

She sipped her coffee, keeping her eyes glittering with amusement on her former cowhand.

"We're in a pickle, Maggie."

"You are, Bryce."

Adams stretched his arm across the table, placed his right hand over her left one, which felt like parchment stretched over knobby bone. "*We* are."

"We are? Then you must know my man shot your deputy, that worthless Dempsey scoundrel, in self-defense."

Adams removed his hand from hers. "Oh, hell—of course I do!" He'd known that Dave had made the first move even before he'd pointedly asked the banker, English, who'd made the first move and was given a cold, silent stare in response.

"The only trouble *we* have, Bryce, is if you try to arrest him."

"He's gotta come in. I'll make sure he's well represented."

"By Burt Malloy? Hah!" Malloy was the county defense attorney.

"There has to be a trial."

Maggie gave a shrewd grin. "You got Reginald English breathing down your neck."

"Soon, I'll have Aidan Dempsey breathing down my neck, as well."

"So you want to bring my man into town and have them breathing down *his* neck, which you know as well as I do they'll stretch with fresh hemp not a day after he arrives to fanfare around the town gallows!"

Adams planted his right elbow on the table, cupped his thumb and index finger around his mustached mouth, and gazed in perplexity and frustration at his dark-eyed, black-haired former employer. Maggie stared back at him fatefully, challengingly, wondering how he'd play it—like the honest and dutiful young man he'd soon become at the tutelage of his two hardworking, no-nonsense former employers? Or like the man who after eight years as the town marshal of Cimarron and his own hard luck—his wife divorcing him three years ago and taking their two children with her to Denver—had become?

Rachel had found another man but only after finding Adams with another woman, the sad but alluring Angela, whom he'd met at a barn dance, of all places, when he'd been patrolling the crowd for belligerent drunks.

"Where is he?" Adams wanted to know.

"I won't tell you that, Bryce."

"The law would say you're harboring a fugitive, Maggie."

She smiled with genuine amusement. "Are you going to arrest me, Bryce?"

"Dammit, Maggie."

She pursed her lips and continued staring back across the table at him.

He cursed, finished his coffee, set the empty mug back down on the table, and donned his hat.

"Stay for lunch? I chopped a chicken to fry. I remember how you liked my fried chicken. Clara's not here. She rode out late last night and I haven't seen her since. But you know how she is. Probably got on the trail of a big elk and couldn't leave it."

"As wild as ever. Almost like she was born to this country."

"It's her sanctuary from unhappy memories."

Adams nodded. "Thanks for the invitation. I best get Dave back to town."

He rose from the bench with a grunt and headed for the door.

He stopped when Maggie warned, "Don't go after him, Bryce. He's no man to mess with. That's why I hired him."

"I know his reputation." Adams continued through the door, across the porch, and into the yard.

He mounted the gray and, trailing the dun, rode back in the direction in which he'd come, his mind awhirl with all aspects of the problem at hand, and with the question of whether he was any longer the man to handle it.

And how to resolve the issue without getting himself or an innocent man killed.

"Oh, hell!" he said an hour later, when he saw a line of riders crossing a canyon below the forested slope he and his horses were descending.

He couldn't see them clearly, obscured as they were by the trees on the slope, but there appeared to be five or more in the pack. They could be range riders from one of the area ranches, but Adams doubted it. At this time of the year, cowpunchers usually rode alone or in pairs, and they weren't in such a hurry unless they'd gotten wind of rustlers in the area and were heading out to throw a necktie party, to help a pine or two bear fruit—the human kind.

The riders disappeared beneath the belly of the slope, but the fast thuds of their horses' hooves continued, growing louder.

Adams sighed, held Cimarron's reins taut in his gloved hands, waiting. Hearing the riders approaching, still out of sight but climbing the mountain toward Adams. Both his horses were nervous, staring off down the slope, ears pricked, giving quick, nervous switches of their tails. Dempsey's lineback whickered.

Adams saw the crown of the lead rider's hat first. Then Aidan Dempsey's broad, red, craggy face appeared, jouncing with his horse's harried stride. He was a big man with a big, hard gut, clad in a plaid shirt under a buckskin jacket with whang strings jostling from the sleeves. He wore the cuffs of his canvas trousers stuffed down into the mule-eared tops of his boots.

Long, snow-white muttonchops framed his savage face and blue eyes blazed from deep sockets under heavy, snow-white brows as his gaze found the rider ahead of him, and he held up one, gloved hand, slowing his own cream stallion and indicating to those behind him to slow theirs, as well. He had a nose like a wedge, and his nostrils flared and his upper lip rose from his teeth in a doglike snarl. He slowed the big stallion still more until he reined to a stop ten feet from the Cimarron town marshal, curveting the big cream, which kept moving its feet, snorting, shaking its head, sensing the enervation of its rider, which was catching.

The others halted their horses spread out behind their boss—all Dempsey riders whom Adams recognized from town, for most frequented the saloons and parlor houses every weekend. Adams had locked up each a time or two for drunk and disorderly or for slapping around a whore. Dempsey's foreman, Creed Morgan, riding up to his gray off his boss's right stirrup, had gotten especially drunk one night and had threatened to cut the ears off the madam of the Midnight Oil parlor house, and Adams had had to ram the butt of a shotgun against the back of the man's head, which had laid him out for two days.

Dempsey had ridden to town himself to bail the man out of Adams's basement cellblock.

That had been three years ago, before Rachel and the kids had left. But neither Dempsey nor Morgan had forgotten that nasty bit of business. Adams hadn't, either. He wondered now if he still had it in him to do that now—to blow the wick of Dempsey's formidable, dark-eyed foreman to save a whore.

He doubted it. As it was, his hands were sweating inside his gloves, and his heart was chugging. He wanted a pull from his bottle in the worst way.

Dempsey's blazing eyes were on the packhorse. "That him?" he asked sharply, turning those fiery blue eyes on the lawman. His big chest was rising and falling heavily as he breathed. "Is that my son?"

"Sorry, Mr. Dempsey."

"You're sorry? You're *sorry*?" the big rancher snapped. "What I want to know is why is his killer not slung over the back of his *own* horse?"

Adams hesitated. "I thought I'd bring Dave to town, get him to the undertaker, before I rode back out to talk to the man."

"The Nordic?"

"Yes."

"So, he is the one who shot Dave? English sent a man out from town to tell me. Seems my *other* son can't be troubled."

Adams didn't know how to answer that. He himself couldn't understand a brother, no matter how badly he was hurting, not riding up here to fetch his brother's body back to his family ranch, but there you had it. Lon was scared. The Nordic had busted his beak, and that can rock a man back on his heels. Lon was scared of the big Norski because he'd gone up against him, knew what cut of man he was. Yeah, he was scared. Scared like a man who's looked into a grizzly's eyes. And, knowing his father as well as he did, he was afraid of his father, too.

Fear laid over fear could be damn near paralyzing.

Adams knew it all too well himself.

Dempsey's glittery gaze—the man was so enraged he was damn near sobbing—was like two branding irons searing Adams to the quick. Damn, he wanted a drink!

"Sir," Adams said, hating the wheedling tone of his voice. "Dave made the first move. He was going to shoot Nordic. Nordic was just—"

"I don't care! Dave was trying to arrest him, and he resisted arrest. That's what the man English sent out to the Crosshatch told me."

"Yes, but…"

"But *what?*"

"Why don't you let me ride up, try to find him, talk to him? I think I can convince him to ride on down to town with me, give a statement."

Dempsey laughed without mirth. "A *statement*? He killed my son, and you want him to give a *statement*?" He leaned far out from his saddle, his white mutton-chops standing out in stark contrast to the apple red of his weathered cheeks. "The man needs to be *arrested*, Marshal! He needs to stand trial and *hang* from a *gallows*! Do you realize what his getting off scot-*free* could do to my *reputation*?" The rancher shook his head and regarded Adams with bald disdain. "I'm not a weak man, Marshal. As I remember, you weren't at one time, either. A few years ago, you'd have that man in chains by now." He paused. "What the hell happened to you?"

Again, he shook his head.

"Where is he?"

"I, uh…" Again, hating himself for his spinelessness, Adams hesitated. "I don't know."

"What? Maggie Rae didn't tell you. She knows. You visited the Flying W, didn't you? That's where you're coming from!"

"Yeah, but…she wouldn't say. Give me some time, Mr. Dempsey. I know that country. I'll find him…talk to him…"

"Talk to him?" Dempsey scoffed. "*Talk* to him, my ass!"

"We'll talk to him." This from Morgan, who was leaning forward in his saddle, grinning, taking a rare delight in Adams's squeamishness. "You leave it to us, Adams. We'll talk to him just fine. You ride back to town, hide an' watch!"

"Take my boy to town, get him in a coffin," Dempsey ordered Adams. "One of my men will fetch him shortly." He glanced at Morgan and the other men flanking him. "Come on, boys!" he barked.

He reined his cream around Adams and the packhorse and put the steel to him. The others, casting smirks at the disgraced town marshal, followed suit. The thudding of their hooves dwindled quickly as they continued toward the Flying W headquarters.

Adams drew a deep breath, let it out slowly.

He hoped Maggie was ready for them.

God, he hoped she was ready.

CHAPTER SEVEN

E arlier that morning, Anders woke with a start, jerking his head up off his pillow.

Curled up against him under a thick quilt and a mountain lion skin, Clara groaned and opened her eyes, frowning at him curiously through the screen of her mussed, brown hair. "What's wrong? Riders?"

Anders tossed the covers aside and, clad in just his longhandles and wool socks, walked a little uncertainly, still foggy from sleep after the long previous day, to the window to the right of the door. He crouched to peer out. The sun was up, the sky blue. He was usually up at the crack of dawn, but the bed had felt good as had the woman he'd shared it with.

He didn't normally mix business with pleasure, but Clara was a hard lady to deny. And a man had his needs.

Finn lay on the blanket on the porch littered with tufts of fur and bits of bone from a rabbit he'd caught for an early breakfast. The dog was awake and looking around, undisturbed.

Yawning, Anders turned to Clara, shook his head. "No riders. Dreamed I heard someone approach but if anyone was out there, Finn would have let us know. Nice to have a dog about the place."

Clara smiled. "Nice to have a woman about the place?"

Nordic returned her smile with a warm one of his own. "This woman here."

Clara hooked an arm behind her head, leaned back against it. "He's taken to you, Finn."

"He's a good dog. Handy up here...especially now."

"Where are you going?"

Anders had grabbed a towel off a hook in the kitchen and a small soap tin. He'd stomped into his boots and was heading for the door at which he lifted his Winchester from where he'd leaned it against the wall. He smiled over his shoulder at Clara. "Bath time."

She shuddered and hugged herself. "So cold!"

"Wakes a fella up."

Shouldering the rifle, Anders went out onto the porch. Finn rose from the rumpled blanket, watching his new master expectantly, ears pricked. No, not master, *partner.* The collie was not a dog any man could master. Anders suspected the dog had been alone his entire life till now. Like Anders, he was a loner. But even loners needed companionship now and then, especially when they'd found a like-minded partner.

Anders drew the cabin door closed then moved down the steps and into the yard. "Gonna take a wake-up swim," he told the dog. "You can come if you want."

The dog gave a yip and ran down off the porch and ahead of Anders, glancing frequently back at his new partner, eager to learn the man's ways. Anders and the dog moved up and over the bench then down the slope and into the shallow canyon in which the creek meandered, the aspens and pines rising along the incline on the other side of the water, the aspen leaves and pine needles glinting in the soft, golden light, the brown water flashing as it rippled over and around rocks. It made a pleasant, musical sound but not so loud as to cover the sound of possible approaching riders.

The dog following close on his heels now, Anders walked upstream for about sixty yards, until he came to a pool that cut a horseshoe shape into the near bank. His swimming hole. A fishing hole when he found himself with a hankering for mountain trout.

He laid the rifle over a rock, set the towel and soap tin on top of it, kicked out of his boots, skinned out of the longhandles and, stretching his lips back from his teeth, stepped into the pool, the chill water rising to just above his belly. Instantly, goose bumps rose across his chest and broad, hub-like shoulders.

"Oh, that's cold!" he said.

The dog sat on the shore, watching him, tilting his head from side to side, incredulous, mewling deep in his throat. What in blazes was this man doing?

Anders laughed at the dog's perplexity then sank

back into the water, dunking his head then coming up, swinging his long hair from side to side. He sat with his back to the bank, letting the chill water engulf him, opening his pores, bracing him. Gradually, he got used to the water until it almost seemed warm. He stood in a shallow area and soaped himself thoroughly, cleaning away the trail grime.

Suddenly, he felt a prickling sensation across the back of his neck, as though he were being watched.

Finn mewled quietly.

Anders turned quickly. Clara stood by the dog, a blanket wrapped around her shoulders. She smiled as the morning light glinted in her hair. She wore her Stetson and boots, nothing under the blanket, Nordic could tell.

"You are a caution, Nordic."

Nordic laughed. "Been called worse but by none as pretty as you."

She blushed at that and looked down.

He frowned as he rinsed the soap away. "How is it you can sneak up on me? Nobody sneaks up on Anders Nordic."

The dog was sitting again, shuttling his ever-curi-ous, slightly ironic gaze between the two people. It hadn't taken him long to warm up to Clara. Of course, the bone had helped just as one had helped Anders.

She shrugged a shoulder partly exposed by the blanket slipping down that arm. "I hunt. You're not much of a success if you're banging around in the brush."

"Join me?"

She looked at the water and grimaced. She pondered it for a while then stepped up to the edge of the pool. She let the blanket drop. Oh, what a vision, Nordic thought. She let him have a good look at her perfect, high-breasted figure before she stepped off the bank to join him, giving a squeal just before her head went under.

Clara didn't stay long in the pool. Anders was accustomed to the bracing water. She rose and used his towel to dry herself, shivering, then tossed the towel to him when he climbed up out of the stream.

"Race you back to the cabin," Clara said, wrapping her blanket around her shoulders.

Naked, Anders stepped up to her. "Not so fast."

He pulled the blanket off her shoulders and it dropped.

His heart twisted with an ancient male yearning.

She looked down at his waist. Her eyes widened. She smiled and took his hand and they lay together in the soft grass awash in golden sunlight, the heat now beginning to temper the chill of the morning air.

The dog watched, baffled.

———

After breakfast, Anders and Clara saddled up and headed toward the Flying W. Anders wanted to check on Maggie. He didn't want Aidan Dempsey taking out on her what Anders had done to the rancher's sons.

"He won't do anything to Maggie," Clara tried to

assure Anders as they headed north out of the higher mountains. "She has many friends in the Chamas. If he did anything to her, it would ignite a war."

Anders nodded but he wasn't so sure.

He and Clara didn't follow any particular trail but headed cross-country via a route Anders had chosen because he believed it would not be as apt to hold tracks. To make it even harder for someone to back-track him, he and Clara traced a somewhat circuitous route, staying mainly in rocky canyons until, in the early afternoon, they climbed a pass between stone outcroppings and started down the opposite side toward the Flying W headquarters.

Finn had been following the pair but took frequent side trips to hunt rabbits and squirrels that chittered angrily at the dog from trees. Now as they headed down the pass, Finn stopped suddenly and, gazing off to the northeast, raised his hackles and showed his teeth.

Anders and Clara checked their horses down and peered toward where the dog was staring, growling softly.

"Easy, boy," Anders ordered. "Easy, now."

Then he saw what the dog had seen—two riders riding through a wash a couple hundred yards away.

Clara saw them, too, and sucked a sharp, startled breath.

"Come on!"

Anders reined Apache into the thick forest on his left. Clara followed suit, and instinctively knowing to stay quiet, Finn followed in silence, glancing back over his shoulder toward the two riders as he did.

Anders steered Apache around a moss-pocked escarpment in the forest then stopped and dismounted on the opposite side of it. Clara did, as well, both riders shucking their rifles from their saddle scabbards. Anders fished a spyglass out of a saddlebag pouch then, Clara and Finn both striding along beside him, walked back around the scarp to the edge of the trees.

The two riders had stopped their horses and were facing each other, talking.

"Think they saw us?" Clara said.

"Not sure. I think one turned toward us just as we entered the trees."

Anders dropped to a knee, unsheathed the spyglass, and gazed through it, adjusting the focus until a clarified sphere of vision swam into view. He studied both riders then handed the glass to Clara.

"I don't recognize either one, but then I never see anyone out here and I only get to town once a month. You take a look." She didn't get to town as much as he did, but she'd been in the country longer.

Clara held the brass-framed glass to her eye, peering out around the side of a large pine.

Finn sat nearby, whining softly, sensing the humans' anxiousness.

Clara lowered the glass. "I've seen them both on the range. I don't know that dark-haired man's name, but he used to ride for a rancher here in the mountains. The blond one in the cream hat is Blaire Willis. He owns a saloon in Cimarron." She looked at Anders. "He used to ride for Aidan Dempsey."

Anders ran a pensive gloved thumb along his jaw. "We'd best assume they're here for me."

"Dempsey wouldn't have put a bounty on your head already."

"Don't know. Maybe these two want to get a jump on it. Dempsey will likely reward handsomely any man who drags me, dead or alive, back to the Crosshatch."

Clare looked at him again, gravely. "What are you going to do?"

Anders returned her stare with a grave one of his own. "I don't want them backtracking us to the line shack."

Clara nodded as she gave him back his spyglass.

Anders dropped to a knee before Finn. "You can come with us, boy." He wrapped his hand around the dog's snout. "But you have to be quiet, all right?"

The dog stared back at him with his dark brown eyes. Anders thought he saw the cast of understanding in the dog's intelligent gaze. Finn lifted one paw, brushed it across Anders's wrist, gave a very quiet yip, then lowered the paw.

Anders turned back to the riders he had to assume were a threat. They'd disappeared around a bend in the canyon wall, heading roughly south, the same direction in which the line shack lay. Anders pouched the glass and dropped it inside his shirt to hang from his neck by a leather thong.

To Clara, he said, "We'll leave the horses. Let's go."

———

Anders, Clara, and Finn quietly crept over the shoulder of the pass, concealing their movement with rocks and trees, making sure they couldn't be seen from the wash.

Anders had ridden this way before, so he knew that the mouth of the wash lay roughly a hundred yards north of his and Clara's position. The two riders would likely ride out of it there.

He, Clara, and the dog strode with cautious purpose, trying to make as little sound as possible. Finn was a smart dog. He knew what the humans were doing, and he made even less noise than they did.

Anders saw the mouth of the pass just ahead, the cut climbing behind rocks on his left. He and Clara slowed their pace. Anders held up a hand to tell Clara to wait behind him with Finn. Then he edged a look around a rocky dike sheathing the wash as it rose from its cut.

He gazed along the meandering floor of the wash, frowning.

No sign of the riders.

He waited, watching, then turned to Clara, who arched a curious brow at him.

Finn was no longer by her side.

Anders looked at the ground rising out of the wash,

and his heart skipped a beat when he saw where a shod hoof had scraped a rock. He spied a hoofprint in the gravel. As he did, a shadow slid across the ground beside him. He jerked a look up at another scarp rising behind him just in time to see a man's silhouette straighten at the top of the scarp, raising a rifle to his shoulder.

"Got him!" the man said.

"Clara, down!" Anders yelled and rammed his right shoulder into her, sending her flying with a muted cry, dropping her own rifle.

Anders threw himself to the ground just as the rifle of the man on the scarp thundered, the bullet spanging off a rock near where the big Norski-blooded man had been standing half a second earlier. Anders rolled and sat up, levering a round into the Winchester's action and squeezing the trigger, the trusty repeater bucking back against his shoulder.

He fired once more. His assailant stumbled back, screaming.

He stumbled forward with another scream, dropping his rifle and following it down the face of the scarp, turning a somersault before landing with a resolute thud on his back.

In the corner of his left eye, Anders saw the second man step out from behind a boulder, squaring his shoulders and aiming his own rifle. Anders felt a cold stone drop in his belly. The man had him dead to rights. The man's rifle barked. However, Finn fouled the man's aim when the collie leaped, closing his jaws around the man's right arm, growling and snarling.

The man screamed and fell, grasping his rifle, his

face a mask of pain and exasperation, losing his hat, his coarse blond hair obscuring his face. The man sat up and aimed his rifle at Finn, who was about to lay into him again.

Anders's and Clara's rifles spoke in unison, their two separate bullets punching into the man's chest and laying him out shivering as he gave up the ghost.

Growling, hackles still raised, Finn walked up to the dying man and lifted his leg.

CHAPTER EIGHT

Maggie Rae was swabbing the kitchen table with a bucket of soapy water and a sponge, drawing on a cigarette, when one of the horses in the corral whinnied.

One knee on the bench on the kitchen side of the table, she stopped and lifted her chin to peer out the window on the table's other side. One of the five horses in the corral, a smoke gray stallion named Rocinante—Clara, a reader, named all the horses—stood with his head and tail up, staring toward the ranch portal with its high, wooden crossbar with *FLYING W* burned into it as well as the brand on each end. Sure enough, six riders were just then trotting through the portal, under the crossbar, led by none other than the big-gutted blowhard himself, Aidan Dempsey on a big cream stallion.

Maggie was alone at the headquarters, as her three elderly hands were working the range, moving herds.

Pure anger and aggravated meanness had swollen

the big rancher's big, chunky body to nearly twice its normal size. His big, red, craggy, white muttonchop-framed face, as well.

"Maggie!" the man yelled as he approached the cabin, his stentorian shout rising above the clomping of six sets of hooves. "Maggie, I know you're in there. I need a word!"

Maggie tossed the sponge in the water bucket, toweled her hands dry, then rose onto the toes of her worn stockman's boots to pull her 1860 Henry repeating rifle down from the hooks above the door. She didn't need to check to see that it was loaded. It was always loaded. An unloaded gun was as much good as an impotent man, which is to say no damn good at all.

She racked a round into the action, took one last puff off the cigarette stub clamped between her lips, removed the quirley from her mouth, opened the cabin's front door and flicked the stub into the yard. She crossed the stoop in two forthright strides, and stood at the top of the steps, casting an insolent sneer toward the six riders sitting their fidgety horses roughly twenty feet off the stoop's bottom step, Dempsey and his thuggish foreman, Creed Morgan, flanked by the other four.

"Well, look what the cat dragged in!" Maggie sang out in her customary screech that made every man jack of her visitors flinch, including Dempsey himself. "About time you're getting here, Aidan. If it was my boy that swallowed a pill he couldn't digest, I'd have been here at first light. Hell, it's goin' on two o'clock!"

In the corral on the opposite side of the yard, Rocinante whinnied.

The horse of one of Dempsey's riders answered in kind.

"Shh, shh," the man said, drawing back on the mount's reins.

Dempsey hardened his jaws and lifted his chin. He was holding his Winchester across his lap, gloved hands squeezing it as though he were wringing the neck of the man who'd blown his useless son out of his saddle.

"Where is he, Maggie? Where's the cabin?"

"Go to hell, Aidan," Maggie said. "You know that child was born needin' a bullet."

Dempsey pointed at her, said tightly, "I did not come here to endure your scorn, Maggie. You know I don't like you. Never have. You don't like me. Never have. Magnus and I got along. That's why I'm going to ask you—no, *demand* you—tell me which of Magnus's cabins is that crazy, man-killing Nordic in?"

Maggie smiled. She liked nothing so much as a fight. Even when she was outnumbered. She had to admit, though, however vaguely, that she had the respect of most of the other mountain people in her favor, as well as the fact that she was a woman. Few would shoot a respected rancher of the Chamas. Especially the widow of an even more respected, even beloved, man. This emboldened her, though she wasn't sure how far she could push her luck here with the vile Aidan Dempsey. Especially after one of his worthless sons had been killed by one of her own men, no less.

But she wouldn't give an inch. It wasn't in her to do so. Not even for Dempsey, who everyone knew was responsible for the deaths of many men—rustlers, nesters, free-grazers, rival ranchers, and businessmen.

"Like I said, go to hell. I'll never give him away. He was defending himself. Your hardtail no-account was gonna shoot him out of *his* saddle. Nordic would do what any of us would do. He just happened to be faster than Dave. That quiet Norski is good with his fists, and he's good with his guns. If I was you, Aidan, I'd turn around, go home, bury your boy, an' forget about the man who made the world a better place by shootin' Dave off his hoss!"

Maggie punctuated that with an even broader, self-satisfied grin, causing two dimples to show in her wizened, Indian-dark cheeks.

Dempsey's blue eyes blazed. They were like two Gatling guns firing invisible bullets at the diminutive ranch woman holding the Henry up proudly high across her scrawny chest.

"Maggie," Dempsey said with menacing quietness, "you've pushed me too far."

"Define too far."

Dempsey glanced at his foreman sitting his horse off the rancher's left stirrup. "Creed. Go up there, take that rifle away from her, and drag her out here by her hair." He glanced over his left shoulder and said, "Kelly, pay out a loop." He turned forward to speak directly to Maggie. "Mrs. Rae has just earned herself a Dutch ride!"

Maggie laughed, belying her inward flinch. A

Dutch ride was a colorful, frontier term for being dragged behind a galloping horse, until every inch of a person's clothes had been ripped off their skin…and a good bit of skin itself.

Creed Morgan smiled at his boss then swung down from his saddle. He dropped his reins and strode confidently up to the bottom of the porch steps. He stopped suddenly when he saw the cocked Henry aimed at his belly, the cockeyed grin on the lady of the Flying W's face.

"You don't think I'll kill your longtime foreman, Aidan?"

Dempsey bunched his lips and flared his nostrils. "No, I don't. Not even you would be that stupid, Ma—"

The Henry's thundering report cut him off.

His horse jumped.

Dempsey could smell the acrid powder smoke.

He gazed straight over his horse's anxiously pricked ears. His eyes widened in shock as his foreman, Morgan, clad in a black vest over a red shirt, turned to him stiffly. Maggie had blown the black hat off the man's head. The man's dark eyes showed a shock of their own.

"Bitch!" he cried as he walked over to pick up his hat and poked a finger through the fresh hole in the crown.

Dempsey had rarely not known what to say.

This was one of those rare times.

"Jesus!" said one of the men behind him, all four trying to get their horses settled down. "She'd do it, too!"

Morgan turned toward Maggie, who was just then loudly racking another live round into her Henry's breech. Hardening his jaws in mute fury, Morgan swiped his right hand toward the silver-chased Colt in the black holster on his right hip.

The Henry thundered again, causing every mounted man and every horse to jerk with starts. The bullet plumed dirt beside Morgan's right foot. The foreman leaped with a start.

"Jesus!" the rider behind him said again, quietly.

Again, Rocinante lifted another shrill whinny from the corral.

Maggie cocked the Henry again, narrowed one eye as she aimed down the barrel. "The next one's gonna drill you a blind third eye!"

Keeping her cheek snugged up taut to the Henry's rear stock, Maggie turned, aiming the rifle at Dempsey. "You want the next one, Aidan?"

Dempsey swallowed.

Maggie said, "You owe me two bullets for teaching your man a lesson!"

Dempsey gazed back at her. His eyes were still bright with anger, but that anger was now tempered by incredulity, a rare uncertainty, even fear. "That was a mistake, Maggie."

"If so, one I needed to make. Just like Nordic needed to blow your worthless son out of his saddle."

Maggie narrowed an eye as she aimed down the Henry's octangular barrel. "I could end it right now, Aidan. If you don't want that—if you don't want me to make Mary Pat a widow, I doubt she could handle the Crosshatch on her own, the way I've kept the Flying W on its feet. You get the hell off my land. *Now!*"

Dempsey's red face turned redder. His eyes brighter.

"Creed, get mounted."

As his foreman set the ruined hat on his head and swung up onto his horse, Dempsey reined his cream around sharply and galloped back toward the Flying W portal. His riders followed suit. Creed rode behind them, casting a menacing stare over his shoulder at Maggie, who kept the Henry aimed at him.

Maggie lowered the rifle and watched the riders as they galloped back through the pines and were gone.

She walked back inside the cabin.

Clara's big cat, Thomas Aquinas, sat on the table, statue-like, tail curled around his big body, staring out the window, canting his head a little to stare after the riders. Maggie returned the rifle to its brackets over the door. She moved to the table. The cat looked at her and gave a single meow. Maggie chuckled, gave the cat a pat, then filled a mug with coffee at the range. She grabbed her makins sack and sat down on the bench facing the table and the window.

She produced a brown wheat paper from the leather sack and began building a quirley.

Her spidery hands shook.

Outside, a dog mewled.

Maggie dropped the wheat paper and the tobacco she'd managed to dribble onto it.

Thomas Aquinas gave another meow, leaped off

the table, and bounded toward the cabin's far end and through the open door of the bedroom the cat shared with Clara.

Boots thumped on the porch. A man's deep voice said, "Stay, boy." A dog whined. A big, blond-bearded man filled the doorway, staring in.

Maggie looked at his severely chiseled but handsome Norski features.

Anders's expression was grim beneath the brim of his felt *sombrero*. He held his Winchester repeater on his right shoulder, gloved hand wrapped around the neck. He moved into the cabin. Clara was behind him. Neither said anything as they both sat down on the bench on the other side of the table from Maggie.

Nordic removed his *sombrero*, set it on the table, smoothed his shaggy hair down on his head.

"Spare a cup of coffee, Mrs. Rae?"

CHAPTER NINE

Maggie gave a vague smile of knowing, sliding her insinuating gaze from Anders to Clara and back again. She rose from the bench and walked to the range. Finn sat in the doorway, staring into the cabin, head high, sniffing the air aromatic with the flavor of the coffee on the stove.

"You heard, I take it?" she said, filling a stone mug with the piping hot brew.

"And saw," Anders said. "We were riding in from the back of the house when we heard the shot, holed up in the brush. Didn't look like you needed rescuing, but we were ready."

"I never need rescuing," the proud woman said, setting steaming mugs on the table before Anders and Clara. "I have Dempsey's respect—now more than ever."

"And his anger," Clara added.

"He has mine."

Anders sipped his coffee, set the heavy mug back

down on the table. "Time for me an' Finn to pull out, Maggie. On the trail down here, we ran into two men likely freelancing for Dempsey. This is only going to get worse."

"Didn't take you for the type to run, Anders."

"For you…Clara. I don't have a choice. If I'm gone, they'll eventually give up looking for me." Anders took another sip of his coffee then said over the smoking rim of the mug. "Or they'll follow me and wish they hadn't."

Damn this trouble, anyway, he thought. He was enjoying that cabin, had expected to remain there until the first snows of winter flew. He knew it was his own damn fault. He was forever having trouble keeping his wolf on its leash.

That damn kid, Sonny.

He looked at Finn staring into the cabin from the stoop. The dog regarded him curiously, ears pricked.

But Anders would do it again. A man had to stand up for the helpless, though Finn had proved he was anything but in certain situations. Namely, when a man was bearing down with a gun on his new trail partner and the lady the dog had come to trust, as well.

No, he had to pull out.

Dempsey would return here, raging with a vengeance fury. He was Irish. Anders knew the Irish. Some were even more hot-tempered than the Viking-blooded Scandinavians. The man would likely burn Maggie Rae's cabin. Both she and Clara were tough. But they couldn't hold off Dempsey and his riders or more freelancers, men wanting to make names for themselves with the powerful Irishman. Maggie and Clara would die for what had started as one small incident in town that Anders had instigated himself.

"If you go," Clara said, "he'll have won."

Maggie gave a gleeful laugh as she troughed a fresh wheat paper between the first two fingers of her dark, wrinkled right hand. "My niece thinks just like her aunty!" She leaned over and kissed Clara's cheek. "They'll be back, yes," she said. "And Dempsey will get a bellyful of lead!" She pursed her lips and hardened her jaws, brown eyes smoldering with raw, barely controlled emotion as she stared across the table at Nordic. "I didn't hire you to turn tail and run at the first sign of trouble! What's more, I don't think that's who you are."

Sitting in the doorway, Finn barked. He didn't know what was going on, exactly. But after the ambush on the trail down here, he knew more trouble was afoot. That had kicked up his fighting, protective spirit.

Anders glowered down at his coffee.

Clara was right. He'd started this fight. He had to see it out.

It was an impossible situation, though. How could he help protect the Flying W if he and Finn were up at the line shack?

"I'll move down here. You two can't be alone."

"Pshaw!" Maggie said, her anger focused on him now. "I'm not afraid of Dempsey! I have three men on my roll. They might be old an' stove-up and can hardly sit a saddle, but they still got the bark on. They'll help protect the Flying W. Besides, I have friendly neigh-bors, and I'm pals with Bryce Adams. I'll keep my men here at the headquarters till the trouble blows over."

"I killed Dempsey's son," Anders said. "Rearranged the other one's face. Hell's gonna pop. I'll stay here, help you, Clara, and your men meet it head on."

"Balderdash!" Maggie said, slapping a hand on the table. "I need a man in that line shack so rustlers don't clean me out. That's where you've been and where you'll stay." She turned to the dog. "You an' Finn."

Again, the dog, excitement glistening in his eyes, barked.

Clara's smile grew. She reached over and squeezed one of Anders's hands. "Don't worry about us. We got the bark on, Maggie an' me. Besides, Dempsey knows what would happen if he burned us out? He'd have a major war on his hands!"

I t was a weary Bryce Adams who rode up to the former livery barn which was now the A-1 Furni-ture and Undertaking Parlor in Cimarron, which the gaudy sign over the large, open main doors announced in large, blood-red letters. The garish sign stood out in sharp contrast to the smell of fresh lumber and sour death that aways emanated from the long, log build-ing's deep, dark shadows.

The place's proprietor, Homer Rankin, sat in a

ladder-back chair to the left of the doors, smoking a
pipe. He was a tall, stoop-shouldered man in his late
fifties, with watery blue eyes and clad in his customary
bib overalls and black watch cap, a bag of pipe
tobacco making a front pocket of the overalls bulge.
He had an open bottle of beer on the ground beside his
chair.

He watched Adams rein up before him, trailing the
horse of Dave Dempsey, with Dave himself stretched
out across the saddle, mild amusement showing in the
undertaker's eyes.

Fresh business.

"Who you got there, Marshal?" he asked and spat
to one side.

"One of my deputies."

Rankin stared at Adams, the amusement leaving
his eyes, deep, dark lines cutting across his leathery
forehead.

"A Dempsey?" he asked.

"Dave."

Rankin puffed his pipe. "You don't say. Does the
father know?"

"He'll be sending someone for him soon. Get him
ready, will you? Oh, and advise his old man to keep
the lid on that coffin. The buzzards got to him. His
brother didn't do what brothers should do."

"I just seen Lon headin' for Aubrey Miller's
place."

"You don't say." Adams scratched his neck.
"Likely tyin' one on." Which was exactly what Adams

wanted to do. "Probably hasn't done a lick of work all day."

"There was, uh, uncertainty in his step," the undertaker said, taking another puff from his pipe and smiling again around the stem.

"No doubt."

Adams dropped Dave's dun's bridle reins then reined his own horse around and kicked him into a trot. Five minutes later he reined up in front of his jailhouse and office. It was still padlocked. He unlocked the door, went in, lit a lamp against the shadows angling across the street and through the office windows. He tossed his hat on his desk and sat down in his chair.

He groaned, leaned forward, resting his elbows on his knees, and rubbed his hands brusquely through his graying, sandy hair. He opened a drawer, pulled out a half-empty, unlabeled bottle, and took several deep pulls in quick succession, groaning against the burn after each swallow. He sat back in his chair, lit a black Mexican cheroot, and sat smoking and sipping from the bottle, hating the feeling growing inside him.

What was that feeling? He'd felt it all the way to town after picking up Dave's body, talking with Maggie Rae, then having his run-in with Dempsey. After their conversation, if you could call it that, the hot-blooded Irish rancher had headed for the Flying W.

Adams felt a burn in his belly in dread of what had happened there.

Was the trouble spreading?

If Dempsey did anything to Maggie Rae and her niece and headquarters and the three old coots who worked for her, a good faction of the other cattlemen in the Chamas would likely take umbrage. There was already no love lost between Dempsey and the smaller ranchers in the Chamas. They saw Dempsey as savage and venal and wanting to drive them out and take their land.

They were aways ready to join forces and stand against him.

If Dempsey took out on Maggie what the Nordic had done to his son, a powder keg of trouble would likely be ignited.

So what was Adams feeling anyway besides dread?

Inadequacy. Fear.

There it was.

He took another burning slug of the busthead.

Somewhere along the way, he'd lost his nerve.

What he should do right now is saddle a fresh horse and ride back up to the Flying W and see how Maggie had fared during her visit with Dempsey. But he was tired and weary and didn't have the strength to make that ride, to see what Dempsey had left of the Flying W. What was he going to do about it, anyway? One man against a good dozen or more of the rancher's riders, most of whom doubled as gun wolves.

A few years ago, he'd have made that ride. His pride and sense of duty would have compelled him to. But all he wanted to do now was get a fresh bottle, go home, sit in his rocking chair, and drink himself unconscious. Angela would be going to work soon. He'd have the house to himself.

His wife's name had no sooner passed through his brain when a carriage rattled up to the jailhouse. A minute later, he heard a soft tread on the stoop. Two soft knocks and then the door opened, and Angela's face, framed by her freshly washed and brushed blonde hair, peered at him through the one-foot crack.

She stepped into the office clad in a maddeningly low-cut cream dress revealing her shoulders and most of her bosom. A long slit ran up the side of the dress, showing one long, creamy leg. She wore a brown shawl against the chill that was sliding down from the mountains as more of the peaks were cast in shadow.

"I was wondering if you were back yet," she said softly, glancing at the bottle on his desk. "How did it go?"

Adams shrugged a shoulder. "I hauled my deputy to the undertaker," he said with a sigh. "That's enough for one day."

"Will there be trouble?"

Adams gave a grim smile. "Oh, yes."

"You're drunk."

"Oh, yeah." Adams saw the glassy gleam in her own, jaded eyes. "So are you."

"It's hard to do what I do sober."

"Me, too."

She moved to him quickly and dropped to a knee, the other knee rising through the slit in her dress. "Oh, Bryce—let's leave here. We've overplayed our hand here. It's time to go...while we still can. Before you're..."

She let her voice trail off.

"Before I'm what? Shown for the fool I am?"

"I wasn't going to say that. I was going to say before you're killed."

He wanted to say he was dead already, but it would have sounded too melodramatic even for a dance hall girl.

"Let's go to Albuquerque. Las Cruces. Hell, we could go to San Francisco and start over."

"On what?"

She just stared at him. The implication was clear.

"On your father's money?" he said.

"He wants us both out of town. We're an embarrassment to him. He'd give us all the money we needed just so he didn't have to see either of us—" She stopped suddenly. Tears had come to her eyes. Her voice breaking, she finished with, "So he didn't have to see either of us again."

Adams smiled and tucked a lock of her hair back behind her ear. "Honey, we do each other proud." He pulled his hand away, took another pull from the bottle. "But I'm not ready to run yet. I have to play this out...if it kills me. I'm not man enough to face what I'd become if I ran from this Nordic fellow and Aidan Dempsey."

"Oh, Bryce."

"I know. Maybe in a month or two. But we'll have to do it on our own."

"Why?"

"Because of that look in your eyes when you look at me."

Angela rose, pushing off his knees. "I'm afraid, Bryce. I'm afraid you're going to leave me alone."

"You'll find someone else."

"I know you don't believe me, but it's you I love."

Adams stared up at her. He'd be damned if she didn't mean it. The notion almost made tears come to his eyes.

Amid the dwindling light of the late afternoon, Adams heard a wagon rattle up to the jailhouse. He lifted his chin to peer through the window above his desk and cursed. Aidan Dempsey was climbing down from a buckboard wagon, one of his hands remaining seated, holding the reins. A wooden coffin was in the wagon's bed.

"Adams?" the rancher's raspy voice called out, pitched with customary belligerence. "You in there, Adams?"

Boots thumped on the stoop.

CHAPTER TEN

There was no knock on the jail office door before the door opened and the big, leonine rancher, Aidan Dempsey, filled the doorway, big-gutted and broad chested. His eyes blazed. They boldly, luridly inspected Angela standing near Adams, and the man gave a wry chuff.

"Am I interrupting anything?"

"I was just leaving." Angela glanced at Adams as she headed for the door.

Dempsey stepped aside, his eyes once more raking her brashly, and then she was gone.

"Nice-looking girl," the rancher told Adams. "If she were my wife, she'd be wearing more than that."

He moved forward and slacked into the chair beside the deputies' table, the wood creaking to receive his considerable weight. He glanced at the uncorked bottle on Adams's desk. "Long day, Marshal?"

Adams did not respond but his ears warmed with chagrin.

"They're about to get longer," Dempsey said.

Adams drew a deep breath, held it, let it out slow.

"I came here to implore you to be the professional lawman you once were."

Here we go, Adams thought with an inward wince. *Here we go…*

"I'm going to give you a chance to do your job, so I don't have to do it for you."

"My…job?"

"I want you to ride up into the Chamas and arrest that big Nordic."

Dempsey stared at him, eyes large, cold, commanding.

Adams stared back at him. "What happened at the Flying W?"

"Not enough."

Adams felt a pang of relief. He assumed Maggie Rae and Clara were still alive.

"Didn't hurt a hair on that stubborn woman's head," the rancher said with a cunning smile. "That won't go on forever, however. She'll get the bullwhip eventually. You're friends with the woman. If anyone can get her to tell where that killer is, it's you. Maybe you even know. You once worked that crazy country. You probably know where all three line shacks are."

"I don't."

"Well, find out."

"You know Maggie. She won't tell me."

"Find out," Dempsey said, louder. He jutted a thick, slightly crooked finger at the lawman. "You find him and arrest him, bring him down here to stand trial for Dave's murder and his assault on Lon. You do it, so I won't have to. You know what'll happen if I have to."

Ah, Adams thought. So this is what this is all about. The rancher ran into trouble at the Flying W. He's feeling desperate. He knows what will happen if he does anything to Maggie and Clara by way of locating the Nordic. The other small ranchers will revolt against him, and he'll have taken a tiger by the tail. He has a good dozen men. But the other ranchers, taken together, probably have twice that. If they rode against him, he'd likely be facing an existential threat.

So he wants Adams to do his dirty work for him, to proverbially save his fat ass.

Again, the rancher glanced at the bottle on Adams's desk. "Stop drinking. Become the man you once were. Ride up into the Chamas and do your job. If not…if I have to go after the Nordic…and you know I will because I'll have no choice…you know what will happen." He shook his head ominously. "Fires, shootings, hangings."

All for the boot-stupid Dave? Adams thought in mute exasperation. *If any man were worth that caliber of revenge, it wasn't Dave.*

"Do your job, Marshal." Dempsey rose from his chair, hooking his thumbs behind his cartridge belt and puffing out his broad chest. "Tomorrow. You do your job. I'll be waiting to hear that you have the Nordic locked up in one of those cages back there, and then we'll send for the circuit court judge." He smiled. "And the hangman."

He turned and strode heavily to the door. He stopped and glanced back at Adams. "Do you know where Lon is?"

"Aubrey Miller's place."

Dempsey's eyes grew hard once more. He nodded slowly, jaws dimpling where they hinged. He strode out the door. Boots thumped loudly on the stoop.

Adams couldn't help giving a devilish little smile.

Presently, the wagon rattled away.

———

Aubrey Miller's place was a pink, clapboard, two-story former hotel wedged between a harness shop and the Acme Saloon, on a narrow side street off Cimarron's main drag.

Tinny player piano music pattered from the Acme as Dempsey directed his driver to swing the wagon up to the hitchrack fronting the hurdy-gurdy house. Six or seven saddled horses lazed at the hitchrack. Shadows moved behind the dimly lit, curtained windows of the whorehouse from which emanated the smell of the "midnight oil."

Walt Harrison stopped the wagon behind the horses and set the brake.

He glanced darkly at his boss as Aidan Dempsey reached into the box behind him and produced a coiled lariat.

"This shouldn't take long," Dempsey said curtly.

Harrison winced inwardly at the bitterness in his boss's voice but also at the lariat in his big hand.

Dempsey stepped off the wheel to the ground and mounted the boardwalk fronting the hurdy-gurdy house. He flipped the latch on the white painted front door, its upper glass panel covered with a thin pink curtain. He stepped inside, finding himself in a large parlor so dimly lit that he could make out mostly only the shadows of the girls lounging here and there with their clientele.

The air was rife with the cloying smell of opium.

Miss Aubrey herself, a former teacher, sat in a brocade rocking chair on the room's far right side, smoking a cigarette with a long, black wooden holder.

"No trouble, Mr. Dempsey," the young woman said. "Please."

Dempsey closed the door behind him. "Where is he?"

The madam, in her early thirties and pretty, thick chestnut hair coiled atop her head, lifted her chin to indicate the ceiling. "Fourth door on the right."

She'd started whoring when the school board had dismissed her for having an affair with one of her older students.

Dempsey turned to the stairs rising on his left.

"Mr. Dempsey?" Miss Miller said.

He stopped, glanced at her.

"No trouble. Please, just take him and go."

Dempsey turned and started up the stairs, the hot breath of anger wheezing in and out of his nose. He gained the second story, strode down the hall. The sound of a man grunting, a woman groaning, and bedsprings straining rose ahead of him, growing louder as he approached the fourth door on the right.

"Oh, god," the girl said on the other side of the door. "Oh…Oh, god…feels so *good*. You're in prime for tonight, my love!"

Lon Dempsey kept grunting. The springs kept sighing.

Dempsey turned the knob and opened the door.

He filled the doorway, staring into the small room lit by a single lantern on a table to the left of the bed, its wick turned low.

"Prime form, my ass!" Dempsey barked.

Lying sprawled between the naked girl's spread legs, Lon turned to him, swollen eyes above his bandaged nose bright with horror. "Pa!"

The girl turned to the rancher whose big silhouette filled the doorway and screamed.

Dempsey moved into the room and slammed the coiled lariat down hard across Lon's back. "Get up!"

"*Ow!* Pa!"

Again, Dempsey hammered his son's back with the lariat. "Get up!"

Lon hustled off the girl. "I'm up! I'm up!"

Dempsey grabbed the man by his left ear and led him to the door. "You're coming with me!"

He tugged painfully on the deputy's ear until they were both in the hall, and then the father led the son savagely by his ear to the stairs then down the stairs and across the parlor to the front door. Gasps sounded throughout the room. Aubrey Miller sucked a sharp breath through her teeth. A man chuckled dryly at the sight of Dempsey leading his pale, beefy, naked son out the front door and across the boardwalk and into the street.

"Walt, pry the lid off that coffin!" Dempsey ordered the driver.

"Uh…what?"

"Pry the lid off the coffin!" Dempsey repeated, still holding Lon by his ear as they stood just off the wagon's tailgate, Lon sobbing with both the pain and humiliation.

"You sure you want to do that, boss? Remember what—"

"Pry the lid off that coffin!"

"Uh…yessir, boss," said Walt Harrison, dropping his denim-clad legs over the wagon's front panel.

He picked up a crowbar from among the paraphernalia in the supply wagon and commenced prying the lid off the coffin. As he did, Dempsey opened the tailgate. He was breathing hard, rage a dragon's breath inside him.

He released Lon's ear then slammed the coiled lariat against his back once more.

"Get up there!"

"Wha…Pa, what's this about?"

Dempsey slammed the lariat harder against his son's naked back. "I said get up there!"

"All right! All right!"

By now, several half-clad girls and half-clad men, some holding whiskey bottles, had emerged from the hurdy-gurdy house, forming a ragged spectators' line

along the boardwalk. They murmured quietly, incredulously among themselves.

Dempsey hopped up into the wagon bed as Walt
Harrison removed the lid from the coffin. The rancher
grabbed the back of his son's neck and shoved his
head down toward the coffin in which the dead Dave
lay, hair mussed, eyes half-open, head turned partly to
one side, a perpetual wince on his lips. His face was so
badly pecked he appeared to have been shot with a
twelve-gauge.

"There—you see that!"

"Pa! Pa!"

"That's your dead brother! The one you left to lay
overnight in the mountains so the buzzards could peck
his eyes out!"

"Pa! I'm sorry, Pa, but I was in a bad way!" Lon
bawled, Dempsey holding his face one foot away from
Dave's.

"*You* were in a bad way? What do you think about
your brother?" Before Lon could respond, Dempsey
said, "And then here tonight I find you diddling a
cheap little whore…while I had to fetch your brother
from town!"

"Oh, god…I'm soo sorry, Pa!"

"You're not. But you will be!"

Dempsey removed his hand from the back of the
younger man's head. He turned to Harrison. "Put the
lid back on."

"Yessir, Mr. Dempsey."

To Lon, Dempsey said, "Sit down."

"What?"

"Sid down."

"Wha…wha…wha…whyyy?"

"You're ridin' back to the ranch with us."

"Let me fetch my clothes first!"

"You'll ride back the way you are!"

From the boardwalk came another sharp suck of a breath through gritted teeth. The murmurs grew louder. There were several spectators.

"But, Pa!"

"Shut up!"

When Harrison had the lid back on the coffin, Dempsey stepped down off the wagon and closed the tailgate. "Let's go," he said.

Lon sat back against the side panel, sobbing into his raised knees.

Dempsey walked around to the front of the wagon, barking, "You won't be comin' to town ever again. You will get all the worst jobs on the ranch until you can prove you're man enough to be a hand. If it takes you till you're a hundred years old, so be it!"

Dempsey climbed up onto the wagon's seat. Harrison released the brake, flipped the ribbons over the horse's back, and they rattled off in the night. Lon's wail echoed.

The crowd on the boardwalk murmured their horror.

There was another sharp breath through gritted teeth.

———

A s the wagon passed him, Bryce Adams stepped out of the shadows fronting the mercantile. He stared after the wagon just then swinging off the side street onto the main drag, heading south.

"That," Adams said, hearing a trill of trepidation in his voice, "is one way to skin a cat."

He took the last drag off the quirley in his fingers then flipped the stub into the street.

"Boy," the lawman said, turning and walking toward the main street, "do I need a visit to the Who Hit John!"

CHAPTER ELEVEN

Nordic and Finn ate supper with Maggie and Clara, and since afterward it was too late to start back to the line shack, they spent the night there, as well.

Maggie announced there would be no "cattin' around" as she didn't run a hurdy-gurdy house, so Clara slept in her room with her cat, Thomas Aquinas, and Anders slept on the braided rug on the living room floor.

By choice, Finn slept outside on the porch. He was too new here to be comfortable inside yet.

Nordic smiled when at one point during the night, Finn joined a distant coyote choir from the porch, sounding as much like a coyote as the coyotes themselves. Anders had a feeling the dog had been practicing his falsetto for a long time, probably since he'd been a puppy likely having left poor conditions on a local farm or ranch or been turned out by his feral mother.

Anders woke to Maggie banging pots and pans around in the kitchen and a sleepy-looking Clara sitting at the table with a blanket around her shoulders, reading a book, Thomas Aquinas curled up on a cushion on the bench beside her. Chagrined that he'd slept later than the women, Anders rose, pulled his pants on, and rolled up his soogan. He drank coffee at the table with Clara, smoking a cigarette, then enjoyed Maggie's hearty breakfast of fresh eggs, fried potatoes, sourdough pancakes with freshly whipped butter and chokecherry syrup, crusty dark wheat bread with butter and chokecherry jelly, milk from one of the Flying W's Holsteins, and more coffee.

Filled to bursting after breakfast, he hauled his soogan and saddle outside and retrieved Apache from the stable, leading the horse to the house and saddling him just off the stoop, Finn watching from the porch's front step. He was sliding his Winchester into the saddle boot when Clara came out, patted Finn as she passed him on the steps, and walked down into the yard. She came up to Anders, rose up on her toes, and flicked the brim of his *sombrero* with her right index finger.

"You be careful up there. Like Maggie always says, keep a finger on your trigger and one eye on your back trail."

Anders took her hand and kissed it. "I aways do."

"I'm glad you have Finn. He'll warn you of trouble before you see it."

"I couldn't agree more, though you do realize he's the cause of all of this."

Clara smiled. "He's well worth it."

On the step, Finn yipped and wagged his tail.

"Besides," Clara said, "it sounds like it was more that banker's no-good son who caused all this."

"You're right."

Anders kissed her cheek then swung up into his saddle. "I hate leaving you two."

"You have to."

"I know. Be careful." Anders hardened his anvil jaws. "If anything happens to you, Dempsey won't know what hit him."

Clara smiled. "Oh, I think he'll know, all right. You're needed at the line shack. Maggie's right—without that chunk of range being overseen, the rustlers will rob us blind."

"I know."

Anders had been up there for four months, and already he'd killed two long-loopers and run off a passel more. Those reaches were peppered with Maggie's longhorns bred with English stock—prime beef.

"All right," Anders said. "Come on, Finn."

As he swung Apache around and the dog came running down the porch steps, tail wagging, Clara said, "Don't be surprised if you have a visitor again some-time in the near future. I rather liked the other night as well as the next morning."

Nordic stopped Apache and turned to the woman. "Don't do that again, Clara. Not now. Too dangerous."

She narrowed an eye at him, spreading her full mouth in a lusty smile. "Like Maggie said, we have the bark on and I now my way around a Winchester."

Anders gave a wry chuff and put Apache into a run, galloping out of the yard through the portal and into the morning's forested mountains bathed in cool, buttery light. Finn ran along behind, barking.

Clara smiled after the big, laconic loner and his half-wild dog, knowing she was falling in love then went back into the cabin to help Maggie with the breakfast dishes.

———

N ordic was halfway back to the line shack when, climbing a forested ridge, he came upon a pile of fresh horse apples. They were so fresh he could smell them from several feet away.

A little farther ahead he came upon the tracks of three horses mixed with the prints of at least five cattle.

Also fresh.

Instantly, alarm bells went off in the big man's head. He shucked his Winchester from its scabbard and cocked it one-handed, looking around carefully. Finn sniffed the apples and then the tracks and looked up at Anders, moaning.

"Yep, you know it, too, don't you, boy? We got trouble." Anders booted Apache forward, continuing to climb the ridge. "Don't take long for the cat to be away that the mice start to play."

He, Apache, and Finn followed a circuitous route

through the forest. When they gained the crest of the ridge, Anders stopped and looked around. Nothing but more sun-dappled forest around him, a canyon yawning on the crest's other side. He'd just started to boot Apache forward when he heard something. He checked the horse down once more and cocked his head to listen.

The sound came again.

Cattle lowing.

His heart quickened.

The lowing was coming from the canyon directly below him.

"Hi-*yahh*, boy!" Anders put the rangy Appaloosa down the next ridge, Finn following close by his side.

He followed the loudening sounds of the cattle to the bottom of the canyon and then into a small side canyon in which five longhorn-English crosses stood, tightly gathered and peering over the makeshift gate of deadfall timber. The cattle were badly upset by their artificial confinement, and so was Anders, who looked around cautiously for their captors before swinging down from Apache's back, removing the timber from the mouth of the canyon, and turning the cattle loose.

They ran off, mooing and bucking their indignation.

He found the tracks of three horses leading away from the box canyon and, rage burning inside him, followed them up the next ridge to the south. He'd climbed only another hundred yards when something curled the air just off his nose to slam into a tree bole twenty feet away on his left. Apache reared, whinnying shrilly, and Anders went sailing off the horse's left hip as the whipcrack of the rifle that had fired the bullet reached his ears.

He struck the ground on his back and shoulders.

Apache swung around and, giving another shrill whinny, galloped back down the ridge.

Anders lay there for a few seconds, groaning, ears ringing from his unceremonious meeting with the ground. He shook his head to clear the cobwebs then, as another bullet pounded the ground to his right, peppering him with dirt and pine needles, he scrambled to his feet and, unholstering his big Colt, dove behind a stout pine bowl.

The rifle's bark sounded once more.

He sat with his back to the pine, waiting for another bullet to carom toward him.

None came.

He turned his head to his left, edging a look around the pine.

Roughly fifty yards away, a gray stone escarpment rose.

Atop the escarpment he saw a man's hatted head, and then the man brought up a rifle and aimed down the barrel toward Nordic.

Anders pulled his head back quickly to avoid being drilled a third eye.

The bullet slammed into the side of the pine where his head had just been, throwing pine bark in all directions.

"That son of a bitch is a pretty good shot for a

rustler," said the big Dakota Norski. He rose quickly to his feet—especially quick for a man his size.

He took off running at a crouch through the pines, weaving his way, climbing up a low ridge and, as more bullets hammered the ground around his scissoring boots, dove over the top of the ridge and rolled down the other side. He rolled up against a tree and, cursing under his breath, rose to his knees. He could see only the very top of the scarp from this vantage. He turned and moved farther down the ridge and swung right and ran, crouching, along the base of the ridge, intending to make his way around the ridge and come up behind it.

As he did, he realized he hadn't heard or seen Finn since Apache had bucked him out of the saddle.

He hoped the dog hadn't taken a bullet.

The low ridge traced a horseshoe shape along the base of the scarp. Near the scarp's rear, the ridge played out and Anders found himself looking up the steep rear wall of the escarpment, which was about a hundred feet high. At least, it appeared that high from here.

To his left, a horse whinnied.

He took several steps in that direction until he saw three horses tied to trees roughly seventy yards away.

The rustlers' mounts.

Anders scrubbed sweat, dirt, and pine needles from his face with the sleeve of his shirt and then located what appeared a corridor or flue carved into the rear of the scarp. He started climbing and spied a cigarette stub on the gravel inside it.

This was the way the rustlers had taken climbing the dike.

Grunting his satisfaction, he continued climbing, grabbing thumbs of jutting rock to each side of him and sometimes crawling on hands and knees when the corridor became too steep for walking upright. The flue curved this way and that and sometimes Anders had to duck under low overhanging rock.

Finally, ahead and above him, he saw sky obscured by pine crowns.

He was almost to the top.

Because of the horse's warning whinny, the rustlers were likely waiting for him.

Continuing to climb, he thumbed the revolver's hammer back and extended it straight out and up, looking for a target. He wished he had his Winchester but the hogleg would have to do.

When he was only a few feet from the end of the flue, a few feet from the crest of the dike, he stopped and shouldered up taut against the rock, slowly raising his head and shoulders to see above and ahead of him.

He hadn't quite gotten his eyes level with the crest of the scarp when a man screamed shrilly—a tooth gnashing, ear-ringing cry of pain and horror. Anders lifted his head to see a man come staggering out of a notch in the rocks on the other side of a small flat area, something big and furry on his back. He had a carbine in his hands and wore a canvas coat and black hat. A loud growling rose above the man's screams.

"Hep!" he cried. "Hep me, boys, I'm bein' attacked by a *bear*!"

Only the beast on the man's back wasn't a bear. It was Finn. The big, shaggy collie was growling and snarling and ripping into the back of the man's neck as he rode the man out of the notch.

"What the hell?" said a man ahead and to Anders's left.

Anders turned to see two more men step out of the rocks, turning toward where Finn was getting the best of their partner. They swung their rifles around.

Anders leaped up onto the flat crest of the ridge, dropped to a knee, and shot both men to his left. As the third man flung Finn off of him then turned his rifle on the rolling dog, Anders shot him, too. The man twisted around to stagger backward, screaming and bringing his rifle up once more.

Anders's Colt spoke again, the bullet taking the man through the dead center of his forehead and knocking him off his feet. He fell without breaking his fall and lay still.

Nordic rose.

Finn gained his feet.

He turned to Anders and wagged his tail.

Nordic walked to him, dropped a knee beside him, and wrapped an arm around his neck.

"If you keep savin' my hide like this, you're gonna make me feel like a tinhorn." He gave the dog an affectionate squeeze. "I do appreciate it."

Finn lifted his snout and gave a low, proud yip.

CHAPTER TWELVE

E arlier, Bryce Adams had sat his dapple gray gelding, Cimarron, on a low knoll sheathed in pines and aspens, roughly a hundred yards from the Flying W headquarters.

Despite his head pounding from the Who-Hit-John he'd swilled in the Who Hit John Saloon the night before, he'd gotten up early, while it was still dark, and he was still drunk. He'd saddled Cimarron and ridden out of town guided by only starlight, a fresh bottle wrapped in burlap residing in his saddlebags. He followed a good wagon trail twisting and turning into the mountains, taking one fork after another, until Crow Creek slid up on his right, touched with the pearl light of early dawn.

It was his intention, a desperate one, at that, to ride to the Flying W and implore Maggie Rae to give him the location of the Nordic's line shack. He'd worked out his argument as he'd ridden into the mountains, taking occasional, hangover-tempering sips from his bottle. He'd try to convince the madam of the Flying W that only he could save the Dakotan's life—by taking him back to town to stand trial. He'd try to convince Maggie that the man would, indeed, get a fair trial. That Adams would summon an honest and fair circuit court judge who was not in the pocket of Aidan Dempsey.

Yes, one existed in Mesilla. The Honorable Jedediah McAffee was an old friend of Adams's, who'd once broken horses for the man on the judge's sprawling Eagle Creek Ranch. On Bryce's request, he'd ride up to Cimarron to oversee the trial.

In the meantime, Adams would have the Dakotan locked up in his jail, safe from the banker, Reginald English, and Dempsey. Neither man would kill Adams to get to his prisoner. Doing so would cause a scandal in Cimarron, where Adams's fairness and honesty, if not his recent battle with bottle fever, had made him many friends who knew him to be the best of the law-bringing lot—at least, in these remote environs, where crooked lawman, susceptible to the bribes of wealthy men, outnumbered the honest ones by ten to one.

The common man—shopkeepers, miners, woodcutters, and freight drivers—would back his play. Dempsey and English knew that.

If Adams didn't bring Maggie's man to town, Dempsey would scour the range until he found him and killed him. Dempsey's dozen-plus men were known gun wolves, and they always got their man—no matter how big and crafty.

Maggie trusted Adams well enough that he'd convince her he was right.

After the trial, when the judge and jury had deemed that the Dakotan's killing of Dave Dempsey had been justified, Nordic could return to the line shack...

Now, however, gazing toward the Flying W headquarters through his field glasses, his location well concealed by trees, Adams began to revise his strategy. Ten minutes ago, he'd watched none other than the Nordic himself lead his big Appaloosa out of the Flying W stable and up to the main lodge, where he'd commenced to saddle the mount.

The big man must have spent the night right here at the ranch's main headquarters!

In a few minutes, he'd likely head back to his line shack.

And Adams would follow him and try to get the drop on him...

Now, as the big man finished saddling his horse, Clara stepped out of the cabin and walked down into the yard. She and the Nordic conversed for a few minutes. There was obviously some intimacy between them.

Adams waited, watching through the field glasses, his heart quickening.

Then, when the big man stepped into the saddle, swung his horse around, and galloped out of the yard to the south, the dog following, barking, Adams quickly sheathed his glasses, dropped them into his saddlebags, and reined his gray down the knoll, in the opposite direction of the ranch headquarters, not wanting to be seen by the Nordic nor winded by the man's dog. He rode around the base of the knoll and swung east, then south, heading cross-country just as Nordic was. Adams waited, letting the man, horse, and dog get a good way ahead and then put his own horse into the rough country to the south, staying well back from his quarry, not wanting to be seen or winded. Such a man would keep a close eye on his back trail and would rely on his dog to alert him to the scent of someone shadowing him.

Adams rode south, climbing higher and higher, following the man's trail, catching only brief, sporadic glimpses of the Nordic himself riding well ahead, climbing the forested ridges on his way to his line shack. Adams climbed one ridge after another, rode through one canyon after another, crossed one creek after another for close to an hour before, after having lost sight of his quarry, guns began blasting ahead of him.

Adams checked his dapple gray down quickly, stepped out of the saddle, and led the horse partway down the ridge and into some aspens, tying him. He fished his field glasses out of his saddlebags, shucked his Winchester carbine from its scabbard, and lay belly down near the crest of the ridge, peering ahead and above him, toward where a gray dike humped up in the forest roughly a hundred yards beyond. He couldn't see much—just the gray blotch of the escarpment and an occasional puff of gun smoke.

Adams scowled through the field glasses, incredulous.

What had Nordic run into?

Dempsey's men?

Adams doubted it. He knew the rancher wanted Adams to have his shot at the man first. Dempsey wanted to do all he could to avoid a range war. Besides, Dempsey didn't know where the Nordic would be headed, unless his men had somehow located the line shack he was occupying.

The lawman doubted that.

Roughly a half hour before, Adams had heard the lows of distressed cattle. That caterwauling had drifted gradually to silence. Now it occurred to the Cimarron town marshal that the Nordic had freed captive beeves. Which meant he'd likely found the men who'd captured them.

Rustlers.

Still, he waited, finding himself half hoping the rustlers would do his job for him—kill the man he was tracking. Of course, such sentiment didn't do much for his pride, but he suddenly realized he didn't have much pride left. All he really wanted was to ride back to Cimarron, have a few more drinks, and go to bed early for a long, dreamless sleep...

Adams stayed where he was, hearing the sporadic gunfire blasting ahead and above him.

Finally, after a good bit of screaming and growling, the shooting dwindled to silence.

When that silence continued, Adams rose and strode up and over the crest of the knoll, walking slowly up the ridge, weaving through the trees. He'd walked maybe thirty yards before he heard the thudding of a horse's hooves and the loud, raking panting of a dog. The thudding dwindled to silence.

It sounded as though the Nordic had won the fight and was continuing toward the line shack.

Quickly, Adams swung around and returned to his horse, dropping the field glasses into his saddlebags. He swung up into the saddle and put the dapple gray ahead and up the ridge, weaving through the mixed aspens and pines. Occasionally, through the trees he caught glimpses of the horseback Nordic and the shaggy collie dog running along beside him. But then, twenty minutes after he'd heard the shooting, he lost the man.

And could not pick up his trail.

Had he realized he was being followed?

Adams rode ahead, his frustration growing, aggravating his hangover.

He rode this way and that along the shoulders of ridges, trying with a building desperation to pick up his quarry's trail, worried he'd lost him for good. He'd once known these mountains relatively well, having ridden up here on the trail of owlhoots on the run, but he hadn't been up here for years. Suddenly, having ridden blindly for nearly a half hour, he found himself badly disoriented, lost.

He stopped the gray, pulled his canteen off his pommel, opened the cap, and took a long pull of the brackish water.

Off his left flank came the metallic scrape of a rifle being cocked.

He pulled the canteen down quickly and closed his right hand over the grips of his holstered .44.

"Easy, now. Easy there, lawman. Don't do nothin' foolish and get a bullet drilled through your fool head."

Adams froze.

Embarrassment raked him. He'd been so intent on the Nordic's trail that he hadn't paid enough attention to his own back trail. He'd let himself get flanked.

By whom?

He turned his head to his left, saw a bearded man in a floppy-brimmed black hat and ragged sheepskin coat crouching beneath a spruce, aiming an old-model Winchester at him. There was a good bit of gray in the man's beard, and his bulging blue eyes regarded Adams shrewdly.

"Who're you?" he asked the man gazing down the barrel of the Winchester at him.

"None of your damn business," the man scoffed.

Rustler, Adams thought. Likely one who'd somehow avoided the Nordic's bullets. He'd likely been following the man, too, with the intention of putting a bullet in his back.

"Nice hoss," the man said.

"What do you want?"

"What do you think? The gray."

Adams said, "Just take it easy." The man had likely seen the badge pinned to Adams's vest. "Like you said…I'm law."

"You think that'll save you from a bullet?"

Adams gave an inward shudder. He could feel the target on his back. It was a large, chilled, circular area, prickling.

Damn fool, he scolded himself. He should have been more watchful. A few years ago…several gallons of hooch ago…he would have been.

Fear was lead in his belly.

He was about to die.

His assailant's silence told him that.

His heart thudded. Heat rose in him. Quickly, panicking, he reached again for the .44 but got it only half out of its holster before his assailant's rifle thundered. The bullet ripped into the outside of Adams's right arm, punching him down the right side of his saddle. He struck the ground on that arm, filling him with burning agony. The gray whinnied, reared, and bolted forward, running off through the forest, reins bouncing along the ground to each side of it.

Groaning, clutching his wounded right arm with his gloved left hand, Adams rolled onto his back. As he did, the man who'd shot him rose from his crouch, stepped out from beneath the spruce, and moved toward him, grinning inside his tangled, gray beard. He wore baggy sack trousers; a Schofield .44 hung low on his right thigh. He aimed the Winchester straight out from his right hip. He ejected the spent round from the rifle's action and stopped six feet away from where Adams lay on the forest floor, groaning and clutching his bloody, upper right arm.

"You kill me, you'll hang," Adams warned the man.

"I don't think so," his assailant said. "The great thing about these mountains is they're remote. No, no...I don't think anyone's ever gonna see you again. No one but the wolves and wildcats, that is..."

He chuckled and raised the rifle to his shoulder, narrowing one eye as he aimed down the barrel at Adams's head.

The lawman watched in dread as the man's right index finger began to draw back against the cocked rifle's trigger.

Adams squeezed his eyes shut.

The rifle barked.

Oddly, it sounded farther away than where the rustler was standing.

Oddly, Adams felt no bullet piercing his forehead.

He opened his eyes.

His assailant fired his rifle into the ground beside Adams, the bullet pluming dirt and pine needles. He dropped the rifle, staggered to his left, twisted around, and dropped to the ground without breaking his fall. He lay with his breath rattling throatily as he died, blood oozing from a ragged hole just above his right ear.

CHAPTER THIRTEEN

S till cupping his left hand over his right arm, Adams stared at the dead man in shock and incredulity.

To his right, a dog barked.

There were the thumps of four running feet, snarls and raking breaths.

Adams turned to see a big, shaggy collie dog running toward him, growling.

A big man stepped out from behind a large-boled pine, racking a shell into the Winchester in his hands. He was big and blond with handsome, chiseled features behind a thick, red-blond beard.

He set the rifle on his shoulder and walked toward Adams, regarding the lawman from under the brim of his cream *sombrero*, the thong of which dangled across his broad chest clad in an only partially buttoned, cambric tunic. Denim trousers were drawn taut across his thick, muscular thighs, the cuffs stuffed into a large pair of high-topped brown boots. A bone-gripped .44 was holstered on his right thigh.

The Nordic.

He didn't look happy.

His blue eyes were hard, cast in disgust.

The dog ran past Adams, sniffed the dead man then came over and sniffed the lawman's bloody arm. He whined and sat down, a statuesque air about him. Adams recognized the dog. He'd seen him prowling the streets of Cimarron several times—a loner, he never ran with the stray packs. In his jaws was usually a dead rabbit or a bone gleaned from a trash heap behind one of the town's several butcher shops.

The dog glanced at the Nordic, who stopped several feet from Adams, casting his cold, hard gaze first at the dead man and then at Adams, those lake-blue eyes studying the man for several seconds before he sighed, shook his head, and said, "You damn fool."

"Should be carved on my gravestone."

The big blond man said, "I should have let him kill you—you know that, don't you."

"Yes," the lawman said, wincing at the hot, throbbing agony in his arm. "You should have."

"What're you doing up here?"

"I wanted to talk to you. You have me in a whipsaw—you know that, don't you?"

"No worse than my own…Maggie Rae's. What am I supposed to do with you?"

"Help me onto my horse. I'll ride back to town…if I can find my way from here. I admit I'm a little lost. I'm not the tracker I once was."

"I don't think you're much of anything you once were."

"Look—either shoot me or help me onto my horse and I'll find my way back to town."

The big man stepped forward, hunkered down on his haunches, removed Adams's hand from the wound to inspect it, then shook his head. "You won't make it. You'll bleed out before you've ridden a mile."

Adams looked at his bloody arm, stretched his lips back in pain and disgust with himself.

The Nordic removed Adams's neckerchief, wrapped it around the lawman's arm, and tied it tight, making Adams groan and wince. "Oh, Jesus!"

The Nordic straightened and began walking toward the crest of the shallow ridge they were on. The dog rose and dutifully followed, sort of whimpering and growling at the same time.

"Where you goin'?" Adams asked.

"To fetch your horse. You wanted to see where I live, didn't you?"

Then he and the dog were gone.

They reappeared about ten minutes later, the dog running ahead of the Nordic, who was leading Adams's dapple gray. The big man stopped the horse beside Adams, dropped the reins, and went over and helped the lawman to his feet. The maneuver along with the blood loss made the ground seem to pitch around Adams, whose vision dimmed slightly, making him feel as though he would pass out.

"Where we goin'?" he asked the Nordic as the big man helped him onto his horse.

"Like I said."

"The shack?"

"Mi casa, tu casa."

"Sure you want to do that?"

"No." The Nordic mounted his Appaloosa and glowered over at the lawman crouched forward in his saddle, wincing against the pain in his arm. "But I can't leave you here to die…you damn fool!"

Leading Adams's horse by the bridle reins, the big man clucked his Appy ahead, moving slowly up the ridge, the dog running along beside him, panting. Twenty minutes later they crossed a creek, rode up and over a bench, and drew up before a brush-roofed log cabin tucked back in the pines. Now Adams knew why the cabin was so hard to find. It was positioned so that you couldn't see it until you were within just a few yards of it. You couldn't see it from the bottom of the ridge and even atop the ridge you might miss it.

Magnus Rae really hadn't wanted anyone to find it.

He'd been an odd, quiet loner before he'd married Maggie, who, with her own big personality, had managed to bring out some personality in Magnus.

The Nordic helped Adams down from his horse and led him into the cabin that smelled strongly of leather, animal skins, and woodsmoke. He eased the lawman into a chair at the small, square eating table constructed of wide, age-silvered, scarred pine planks, then squawked open the door of a small, iron wood-stove and stoked coals to glowing life before adding several slender chunks of pine.

Sitting in the open doorway, the dog watched.

The Nordic grabbed a cast-iron pan off a wall hook and strode out onto the cabin's small stoop. Adams heard the splash of water and then Nordic returned and set the pan atop the range. He grabbed a jug of whiskey off a shelf and set it on the table then produced a rag from another hook and set it, too, on the table.

He saw Adams gazing hungrily at the bottle then gave a dry chuckle and pulled two tin cups off yet another shelf, set them both on the table, half filled one of them, and splashed a little into the other cup.

"A drinkin' man," the Nordic said.

Adams picked up the cup with one shaking hand and downed half the liquor in two gulps. With a deep sigh, he set the cup back down on the table. "Especially when I have a bullet in my arm," he added, defensively.

"I've seen you in the Who Hit John," the Nordic said. "Looking a little glassy-eyed in the midafternoon."

"Oh, go to hell!"

"See ya there." The Nordic raised his cup and threw back the whiskey, winced a little as he swallowed, then set the cup down on the table.

He made coffee and by the time it was done, the water was steaming.

He poured the water into a porcelain basin, dropped the rag into it, then unsheathed his Green River knife, slid up close to Adams, and began cutting off the man's right shirtsleeve.

"You came up here to arrest me?"

"I came up here to convince you to ride with me back to Cimarron. You'll get a fair trial."

The Nordic laughed.

"I'll do everything I can."

"Well, thank you mighty kindly. Not going to happen. You know as well as I do that Dempsey and the redheaded popinjay of a snooty banker would see me hang...with the help of Dempsey's payroll." The big man shook his head. "I'll take my chances up here."

"They'll find you eventually. For God's sake, man, you killed Dempsey's son, gave the other one a permanent bulge in his nose! You can't do that to a man like Aidan Dempsey and not pay for it. If you come back to town, I'll protect you and send for a good, fair circuit court judge."

The Nordic had dropped the bloody shirtsleeve on the floor and had started cleaning blood from the edge of the wound. The wound appeared to have stopped bleeding, which gave the lawman some relief. Maybe he wouldn't continue to lose strength.

"You can't even protect yourself."

Adams flushed at that, knowing it was true. He felt helpless and deeply frustrated. He made some mutterings, trying to find a solution to the dilemma, knowing there was none. He'd thought maybe he'd be able to lead the big Dakotan down out of the mountains at gunpoint, if he had to. But now he knew that had been wild, drunken imaginings.

Deep down, he'd wanted to look tough and no-

nonsense in front of the town including the banker and
Aidan Dempsey.

What a fool he was. The Who-Hit-John must have
pickled his brain.

"Why are you doing this?" he asked the Nordic.
"Why didn't you shoot me?"

"Good damn question."

"I've seen the cabin."

"Seein' it once is one thing. Finding it again is
another thing."

Adams pondered that, more shame burning in him.

He took another big drink of the whiskey, splashed
more into his cup. "He'll find you. His men will scour
these mountains until they find you."

"If so, they'll pay one hell of a price for hanging
me." The Nordic rose from his chair and gave the
lawman a hard, level gaze. "Dempsey will be the first
to be sporting a third eye. One he couldn't see worth a
damn out of."

"Why don't you just leave the country? Head to
Arizona or Mexico for a few years."

"Maggie wants me to stay."

"That stubborn, crazy mountain woman…"

"We don't run from trouble."

It was Adams's turn to laugh dryly. "You're as
crazy and stubborn as she is. As that crazy niece of
hers is."

"You got that right. Us crazy folks have to stay
together." The Nordic grabbed a canvas pouch out of a
steamer trunk in the bedroom side of the cabin. He
returned to the table, set the pouch on it, and withdrew

a small leather wallet. He opened it—inside were a long needle and catgut thread.

"Oh, Jesus," Adams said.

"Have to stitch it closed or it'll open up. You'll never make it to town."

"Not sure I even want to." All kinds of crazy trouble awaited him in those environs.

The Nordic threaded the needle, pinched up the skin around the wound, and poked it through.

"Oh, god!" Adams cried, hardening his jaws and tipping his head far back.

In the doorway, the dog barked.

———

A idan Dempsey stared down at the pale blue countenance of his dead son laid out on the dining room table in his big house at the Crosshatch headquarters.

His wife, daughter, and their housekeeper, a stout half-Mexican woman named Pilar Andromeda, had stripped and cleaned the body and dressed it in the suit Dave wore to church on Sundays. Buzzards had pecked his eyes out. His entire face and neck looked as though he'd been shot with a twelve-gauge. Yes, Dave had gone to church. So did Lon. Aidan Dempsey would have it no other way.

Silent rage burned through Dempsey. His hands hung straight down at his sides, fists clenched.

He was aware of his wife, Mary Pat, and his daughter, Henrietta, sitting behind him in broadcloth

armchairs abutting the dining room's outside wall.
Both were dry-eyed, still in shock. They were dressed
in their best, lace-edged muslin frocks. What was it
about death that made people feel the need to dress up
for it?

Dempsey had, as well—in a black pinstriped suit
with black foulard tie attached to a celluloid collar at
the throat of his best, white cotton shirt. His thick,
white hair and muttonchops still showed the tracks of a
comb.

The heavy-bodied Lon sat in another armchair on
the other side of Dave's casket from Dempsey. His
eyes were still black, though the swelling was going
down some, the edges of the swellings a sickly yellow
green. Mary Pat had placed a fresh, white bandage on
his lumpy nose earlier that morning.

Lon didn't say anything, just sat back in the chair,
arms hanging down over the chair arms. His legs were
stretched out before him, booted feet crossed at the
ankles. He glowered at his father like a bear staring out
from a cage.

Soon, the men from the bunkhouse would file into
the house with hats in their hands to slowly shuffle
around the table, paying their last respects to
Dempsey's son, though Aidan knew that not a single
one of them had even slightly liked Dave. Like Lon,
he'd been a lout, make no mistake. Still, he was
Dempsey's son, and he'd been taken away from him.
One certain line shack squatter would pay dearly for
that.

As though she were reading his mind, behind him

Mary Pat said, "What will be done about this, Aidan? We can't have a son killed and buried unavenged."

A plain-faced woman with gray in her lusterless brown hair and a body going to seed, Mary Pat had come from a family of tough, frontier ranchers who, originally from Texas, had settled not far from the Crosshatch headquarters not long after Dempsey himself had pushed a herd up from Oklahoma. All of her brothers and even her father had fought in the War between the States. All had returned alive after Appomattox, though one brother, a sniper known for his savagery, had returned without an arm and one eye.

They were a roughhewn clan, and Mary Pat herself knew her way around the concept of revenge.

"Don't worry," Dempsey said, still staring at his son over whose eyes silver coins had been set. "You'll get your justice, woman." He clenched his fists until his fingernails cut into the palms of his hands. "And so will I. Bryce Adams is looking into initiating it even as we speak."

"Adams is no man."

"No, but he's the law. We have to give him a chance."

A light knock came at the front door in the great room part of the house. Dempsey jerked with a start. That would be the men. He didn't want to see them staring down at Dave's ravaged face, feigning grief and respect.

"I need a drink," Dempsey said, swinging around and heading out of the dining room toward the rear of the house. "I'll be in my office."

Boots thumped on the walnut puncheons of the big house's hardwood floor. Behind him he heard the housekeeper speaking in hushed tones with the men just then filing into the foyer. It was night. The windows of his office were black. The only light came from the charcoal brazier in a corner near his large oak desk. He went into the office, closed the door, and lit a lamp.

He jumped and gave a startled grunt when he saw the silhouetted figure of a very large man sitting in an armchair by a pedestaled stone statue of Robert E. Lee, under the old Stars and Bars hanging on the wall. A large dog sat to his left.

It glared at Dempsey, hackles raised, growling.

CHAPTER FOURTEEN

"Good god!" Dempsey said, holding up the lamp until the guttering light was reflected in a pair of the bluest eyes he'd seen, in a blond-bearded face carved out of granite. "How did you get in here?"

One boot hiked on a knee, the Nordic just stared at him.

The light reflected in the amber eyes of the shaggy dog, which sat with its ears pricked, regarding Dempsey coldly.

The rancher looked at the French door in the wall to his left. The door was cracked. A night breeze stirred the heavy, green velveteen drapes drawn across it.

The big man said, "You must feel rather secure here, Dempsey. Don't you ever lock your door?"

"No man dare trespass on the Crosshatch!"

"Figured you'd think that."

"Do you know how many of my men are less than a hundred feet away?"

"Oh, I'd say all of 'em. When I rode up, I saw them file out of the bunkhouse."

"All I need do is give a yell, and they'll all be here pronto!"

There was a ratcheting click. Dempsey saw the bone-gripped revolver in the big man's hand down near his right knee, the maw yawning at the rancher. It, too, reflected the light of the lamp.

"They'd be too late to save you."

Again, the dog growled softly.

"Easy, Finn," the Nordic said.

The dog stopped growling.

"What're you doing here?"

"Wanted to have a little chat. Sit down."

Dempsey stared at him, angry, frightened, and incredulous. "I don't take orders in my own house."

"Sit down."

Again, Dempsey looked at the revolver in the big man's hand.

He turned and started toward the chair behind the desk but stopped when the Nordic said, "Not there. Over there."

He wagged the gun toward an armchair on the other side of the room from him, under an oil painting of a white, rearing stallion with a wildly buffeting mane and the spirit of the wild in its eyes.

Dempsey set the lamp back down on his desk and, with an angry chuff, walked to the chair and sat down. He sat stiffly, leaning slightly forward, hands on the chair arms, regarding the intruder in silent rage and indignation.

Heavy footsteps sounded in the hall beyond the office's closed door. They grew louder until there came a light tap on the door. A deep-throated voice said, "Boss, me an' the boys would like to say some words over Dave. Would you join us?"

Dempsey turned to the door, heart thudding anxiously. He looked at the Nordic. The big man gazed back at him, warning in his eyes, wry challenge in the curve of his mouth. The dog looked at the door then up at its master and, reading the command, did not growl.

Dempsey turned to the door, heart still thudding. "I'll...I'll be out in a bit, Creed."

"All right, boss."

The footsteps rose again, fading.

Dempsey turned to the big man sitting with annoying casualness on the other side of the room from him. "That was my foreman, Creed Morgan."

"You just saved his hide."

"Why are you here? Say your piece an' leave!"

The Nordic dropped his right foot to the floor and rose from the chair, keeping his revolver aimed at the rancher. He narrowed those blue, blue eyes. "Leave me alone. Leave Maggie Rae alone. Your son deserved what he got. You come after either one of us again, I'll kill you. It doesn't matter how many men you have. I *will* kill you. Now you know how simple that would be."

He looked at the dog. "Come on, Finn."

The Nordic backed toward the door, the maw of the gun still yawning at Dempsey. The big man opened the door three feet, and he and the dog slipped through it. The door closed and latched.

Dempsey heaved a sigh of angry relief, rose, and strode quickly toward the office door. He opened it and yelled, "Creed, have the men saddle up! My son's killer was here!"

————

Outside, Anders Nordic heard the rancher's enraged, thunderous order and grinned.

He removed Apache's reins from the ponderosa pine he'd tied them to and swung up into the saddle. The dog stared up at him curiously.

"Come on, Finn."

Nordic swung the Appaloosa around and rode around the far side of a buggy shed set back in the pines roughly a hundred feet from the rear of the house. He stopped near the shed's corner and leaned forward to gaze around the corner toward the front yard and the bunkhouse on the yard's far side, lamplight in the bunkhouse's sashed windows flickering. A moment later, over a dozen men spilled out into the yard, running toward the bunkhouse. They disappeared into the bunkhouse, ran out a moment later wielding rifles and buckling shell belts around their waists.

They ran to a stable right of the bunkhouse and disappeared into it. Nordic could hear them yelling anxiously as they saddled their mounts. They rode out a few minutes later, the man riding point—likely the foreman, Creed Morgan, yelling toward the house,

"We'll get him, boss! Don't you worry—we'll get him!"

Dempsey was likely standing on the front porch, indignant rage in his eyes.

The angry horde galloped off into the darkness at the eastern end of the yard, whipping their mounts into hard runs with their rein ends, leaning forward in their saddles, hats pulled low over their eyes.

"Well, he can't say I didn't warn him," Nordic said, reining the Appaloosa around and riding through the pines and up a low ridge to the south. "Come on, Finn."

When he was fifty feet from the crest of the ridge, he stopped the Appaloosa abruptly, his hand closing around the grips of his holstered .44, apprehension crawling like a bug along his spine. Then he saw her silhouetted against the starlit sky, hair hanging from her cream Stetson to her shoulders. He removed his hand from his gun, gave an angry chuff, and gigged Apache on up to the crest of the ridge, Finn running along beside him, mewling, happy to see the girl.

Nordic was not.

"Clara, what the hell are you doing here?" he said, keeping his angry voice pitched low as he stopped Apache a few feet from Clara's bay.

"You crossed my trail a ways back,"' she said with annoying casualness. "Had nothin' else to do, so I followed you."

"You damn fool girl!"

She laughed. "*I'm* the fool? You're the one who rode into the lion's den!"

Sitting on the ground beside Nordic, Finn mewled and thumped his tail, staring at Clara, who looked down at him and said, "Finn, at least *you* should have known better. Will you follow him everywhere?"

His body fairly quivering, Finn stared up at her and gave a yip.

Clara laughed. "You would, wouldn't you?"

"Go home, Clara," Nordic said. "I'm taking a roundabout way back to the cabin. Likely won't make it till morning."

"What—you'd leave a girl alone out here to her own devices? I need a big, tough man to protect me."

"The hell you do!"

Again, Clara laughed. "I'll ride with you. Obviously, you need someone to look after *you*."

"Does Maggie know you're out here in the middle of the night?"

"Of course, she does. I'm just like *her*."

Nordic cursed then gigged Apache forward and down the ridge, heading south, though his cabin lay to the east. Clara swung her mount around and followed him while Finn trotted along beside Anders and Apache.

At the bottom of the ridge, Clara rode up beside Nordic and as they continued riding through a broad canyon to the south, said, "What did you hope to accomplish by visiting the Crosshatch? You could very well be dangling from a cottonwood down there."

"I wanted him to know how easy he could die."

"You think you scared him?"

"He was shaking in his boots. Prob'ly changing his drawers right now."

"But he still sent men for you."

"It was worth a try."

"Why didn't you kill him?"

"Too easy."

"Nordic, you're a fool."

"Yep."

"I think I'm in love with you."

"Yep."

"You knew?"

Nordic checked Apache down abruptly and curveted the Appaloosa, facing the woman, who stopped her own horse and looked over at him. "Get it out of your head. I'm not a man to fall in love with."

"You're just the kind of man I'd fall in love with… fool that I am." She smiled, the whiteness of her teeth showing in the darkness.

Finn yipped and mewled deep in his chest.

Again, Nordic cursed and then put Apache on ahead. They rode south for two miles before swinging left to follow and old Indian hunting trail east, toward Nordic's cabin.

They rode in silence for nearly an hour, following the meandering trail which hugged a narrow, aspen-lined creek, before Finn stopped suddenly, lifting his head to sniff the cool night air then mewled and growled, turning his head to stare into an intersecting canyon to his left.

"What is it, boy?" Anders said, pitching his voice low.

But then he heard the distance-muffled thuds of oncoming riders. Soon he also heard the rattle of bit chains and the squawk of tack.

"Back!" Anders said, swinging Apache around and riding into a thick stand of trees near the creek.

Clara and Finn followed and then all three were in the trees, staring toward where the secondary canyon intersected the one in which they were in.

The sound of the riders grew louder until they appeared, jostling shadows in the darkness, tightly grouped and riding south. They passed Nordic, Clara, and Finn quickly and were gone as quickly as they appeared. When the thudding of their horses had faded to silence, Clara said, "Close one!"

"Too close." Nordic's anger rose. "You shouldn't be here. You should be home in bed. If they find you with me…"

"I know what Creed Morgan is capable of. He has a rather seedy reputation in these parts."

"All the more reason you should be home in bed!"

"We've already had this conversation."

Cursing again in deep frustration, Nordic booted the Appaloosa out of the trees and up the trail, continuing east. At least, the Crosshatch riders hadn't picked up his trail. They were riding blindly, hoping they'd run him down by chance. Failing in their endeavor, they wanted to delay heading back to their headquarters and into the wrath of their boss for as long as possible.

They rode for another twenty minutes before thunder rumbled and a chill wind rose, causing goose bumps to ripple along Nordic's back. He looked up. There were no longer any stars. Lightning flashed through a cloud in the west, the direction from which Nordic and Clara had come.

"Going to rain soon!" the woman said as more thunder rumbled, slightly louder than before. "And up here when it rains, it *rains*!"

"Best fine shelter."

"This way!" Clara neck-reined her bay to the south and started up a rocky ridge spiked with pines and firs, the bay lunging off its rear hooves, bit chains jingling.

"Come on, Finn!" Nordic put the Appy up the ridge, as well, Finn running along beside him then running ahead, the wind rippling his shaggy fur. Crouching low against the cold first drops of the rain, Nordic added, "I'll give her one thing—that lady knows these mountains!"

He inwardly admitted he gave Clara more than that. Tough, smart, and beautiful, he'd never known another woman like her. He found his frustration with her waning, but he knew he couldn't fall in love with her. He was no man for Clara. Hunted by Aidan Dempsey, he was dangerous. Besides, he was solitary. Clara was solitary, too, but he was also nomadic. Clara belonged at the Flying W with her aunt.

Nordic followed the young woman up the slope until he saw Clara stop her horse and swing down from the saddle. She led the bay into a gap between cabin-sized boulders. Nordic checked down Apache and led the Appy into the gap, where Clara was just then tying her bay to a cedar jutting out of the side of one of the boulders. As she quickly unbuckled her saddle cinch and set it under a stone overhang of the boulder to which she'd tied her horse, Nordic tied Apache to a small pine, unbuckled his own cinch, removed his saddle, and set it in the shelter beside Clara's.

"Cave up this way!" she said as the rain began slashing down and thunder clapped like war drums.

Tugging her hat brim down against the rain, her Winchester carbine in one gloved hand, saddlebags and bedroll on her shoulders, canteen hanging from around her neck, she ran out of the gap between the boulders and up the ridge. Shucking his '66 from its scabbard and draping his own saddlebags over one shoulder, hanging his canteen from his other shoulder, clamping his bedroll under his arm, Nordic followed the girl up the rocky slope until he saw the dark, egg-shaped mouth of the cave she was heading for. She ducked inside, disappearing until Nordic followed her in, having to crouch low as the cave was maybe only six feet high. Finn was at his heels, growling softly, apprehensively sniffing around.

Ahead of Anders, Clara dropped her saddle, saddlebags, and bedroll, took her carbine in both hands, and loudly racked a shell into the chamber. She swung the rifle this way and that, cautiously looking around, then depressed the hammer and lowered the Winchester.

She glanced over her shoulder at the big man behind her. "Never know what animal might be here," she said, yelling above another thunderclap. "The four-legged kind or the two-legged kind. I've seen signs of both before. Outlaws on the run cool their heels here is my guess. Secret places like this make their way around on the outlaw telegraph is another guess."

Nordic set his saddlebags and bedroll down on the cave floor. "Don't doubt it a bit. It's well concealed. How did you find it?"

"Stumbled onto it while hunting a rogue grizzly feasting on our beef." Clara turned to stare out into the slashing rain and the lightning intermittently lighting up the entire sky. "Rainy night like this one."

Nordic regarded her, incredulous. "Clara, you mean you hunted a *grizzly*?"

The young woman shrugged a shoulder. "Our three hands hunted him, too, but we split up. I found him back down canyon a ways dining on another Flying W heifer. Cleaned his clock with Magnus's old Sharps. That .56 sure had a kick. My shoulder was black for weeks."

Anders laughed and shook his head as he turned to stare out into the stormy night. He gave a little shiver against the damp chill pushing through the cave mouth. It was going to be a chilly night but even if they could secure dry wood, which wasn't likely, they couldn't risk a fire. The storm had probably run the Crosshatch men to ground, but Nordic was not a man to take fool chances. Especially when his wasn't the only life he was worried about.

"Well," he said, plopping himself down on the cave floor, facing the night, crossing his long, muscular legs Indian style, "we might as well make ourselves comfortable."

"I reckon." Clara sank down with a sigh and, resting her Winchester across her thighs, crossed her own, long, slender legs as Nordic had.

Finn shook the rain from his fur then sat to Nordic's left. Mincing his front feet forward, the dog eased himself belly down on the cave floor then crossed his front paws.

The storm expended the bulk of its fury over the next ten minutes. Quickly, the thunder faded into the distance, the rain quit abruptly, the clouds parted, and the half-moon appeared nearly straight up in the sky. Now there was only the sound of the rain dripping from trees and rocks.

"That was fast," Clara said. "Should we continue to the cabin?"

"Might as well stay here. The creeks are likely swollen. They'll go down by morning, which is probably another three hours away."

"The Crosshatch devils are likely heading back to their bunkhouse with their tails between their legs and sad news for their boss."

Clara unrolled her bedroll, slid up close to Nordic, and draped the soogan across their laps. Removing her hat and pulling the stitched-together blankets up to her chin, she rested her head on the big man's shoulder and continued staring out into the night. Nordic wrapped an arm around her shoulders, enjoying the warmth and the supple feel of the young woman against him. Neither said anything. They just sat and enjoyed the night's peace in the aftermath of the storm, gazing up at the moon and the stars winking dimly to life around it as the dark clouds scudded farther and farther apart.

Despite the night's sudden magic, Nordic found himself in a melancholic mood.

He had to admit he liked being here with Clara. She was a special woman. But her presence here, her body pressing lightly against his as he listened to her measured breathing, made him realize what a lone wolf he was. He'd always been so. He realized now that he was a deeply lonely man. Even as a kid growing up in a family, he'd felt alone. It was not in his nature to make friends, no matter how much he'd at times wanted to. He'd grown quickly, and that had set him apart. Others had often looked at him as though he were a monster. Too well he knew the repellent look in others' eyes.

So he had been—a man apart. So he would aways be.

Clara was the first person he'd felt close to since leaving home so many years ago. But he couldn't have her. It wasn't in his nature to remain in one place for long. His was the life of the wandering wolf, avoiding the company of others as much as possible. He knew that Clara knew this about him, and it made him feel sad and lonely for her, too. He didn't doubt that he was likely the first man the young woman had ever felt close to, just as she was the first for him.

Two lonely souls enjoying each other's company for but a brief time.

Anders shook his head as though to clear the self-indulgent thoughts. He was not normally a man to pity himself.

He'd no sooner cleared his mind than one of the horses tucked away in the boulders gave a whinny that sounded inordinately loud in the dense quiet of the storm's aftermath.

Both Nordic and Clara jerked with starts and sat up straight, pricking their ears to listen. Beside Nordic, Finn growled.

Nordic thought the whinny had come from Apache. A rider gets familiar with his mount's warning cry.

Clara turned to Anders. "Company?"

Distantly, another horse answered Apache's whinny with a shrill one of its own.

"Yep!"

CHAPTER FIFTEEN

"Back, Finn!"

Nordic and Clara scrambled on hands and knees deeper into the cave and lay belly down on the cavern floor, both quietly racking rounds into the actions of their rifles. Finn lay behind them, mewling warily. Anders doffed his hat and set it down beside him, then holding the '66 in both hands, lifted his head far enough that he could see down the rocky, pine-peppered slope below the cave.

"Doesn't necessarily have to be the Crosshatch men," Clara said to Anders's right, holding her own rifle in both her gloved hands, thumb on the carbine's cocked hammer.

"Nope. But something tells me it is."

"If so, they're right determined." She glanced at Nordic. "That was a fool thing you did—ridin' into the Crosshatch headquarters. Obviously, you made Dempsey madder'n a stick-teased rattlesnake."

"I reckon I made a slight miscalculation."

"Yeah," Clara said. "Slight."

Minutes passed.

The night was silent. Eerily so.

Nordic felt his heart thumping against the cave floor beneath him as he and Clara stared tensely down the dark slope touched with the milky light of the high-flying half-moon.

"I wonder if Creed Morgan knows about the cave," Clara said quietly.

"Well, if he doesn't, Apache's cry will likely lead him right here."

"The horse was just tryin' to warn us," Clara said, always quick to defend the animals.

"Oh, I know. That whinny has saved my topknot more times than I want to think about. Still..." Squeezing the '66's neck with his right hand, Anders stretched his lips back from his teeth.

It was painful, waiting and listening, not sure if you were being stalked.

More time passed.

From the boulders came the nervous whickers of both horses.

"Dammit, Apache—shut up," Anders said quietly but tautly.

Another agonizingly slow minute passed. Then another.

Clara whispered, "I think I saw something move."

"I saw it. A shadow about halfway down the slope."

"Between that pine and that flat-topped rock?"

"Yes."

That was the only movement either of them saw for another ten to fifteen minutes. Then another shadow moved on the opposite side of the slope from the first one, and Nordic pressed his cheek to the rear stock of the '66, aiming, looking for a target.

"They're coming, all right…and they're gonna get bellyfuls of lead for their trouble." He glanced at Clara. "Dammit, woman—why did you have to follow me? You should be home in bed, safe and sound."

Clara was aiming down the slope now, too. "We've had this conversation. I'm here now. We have the high ground. I'll help you hold them off—maybe even kill a few of Dempsey's demon spawn!"

"Don't get cocky."

Behind them, lying belly down, Finn gave a deep-throated mewl.

There was a bright flash on the right side of the slope, maybe fifty yards down from the cave. The rifle roared, and the bullet kicked up dirt and gravel a foot from the cave's mouth. At the same time, Nordic and Clara returned fire, aiming at where the shooter's rifle had flashed. The whipcracks of the rifles were followed by a man's grunt, the clatter of a dropped rifle, and then the thud of a body striking the ground.

"Jesus!" someone said on the slope.

Behind Nordic, Finn yipped.

"Get 'em!" said another man.

Suddenly, man-shaped shadows were scurrying

around on the slope, weaving between large rocks and boulders as they climbed the incline toward the cave. Nordic glanced at Clara, who gave him a wild, determined look through a crooked grin. Then the two levered fresh cartridges into the actions of their rifles and commenced firing down the slope at the scampering shadows.

There was another scream and then another curse and then a shrill cry as those jostling shadows dropped and rolled. The Crosshatch riders returned fire, but Nordic and Clara had the better angle. They returned fire at the gun flashes, and more of Dempsey's men dropped, a few rising and limp-running or diving for cover.

After only a minute or two, the shadows stopped moving.

Nordic could hear retreating footsteps, cursing, and grunting as the Crosshatch riders reconsidered their mission.

Maybe they should wait until their quarry did not carry the higher ground.

Silence descended along the slope once more.

"Well, well, well," Nordic said, lowering his smoking '66. "How many do you think we got?"

Behind him, Finn growled then barked twice, loudly.

A shadow slid into view to Anders's right and then he saw the bearded countenance of a man stepping into the cave mouth, moonlight glinting off the carbine in his hands. Both Nordic and Clara jerked their rifles up and once more fired simultaneously. The Crosshatch shooter gave an agonized wail as he fired his carbine skyward, stumbling back from the cave mouth then falling, striking the stony slope on his back then rolling wildly for a good twenty feet, piling up against a large, cracked rock.

The man's breath rattled. Gravel clattered as he kicked out his life. Soon he lay still in death.

"I think that's number seven," Clara said.

Nordic turned to where Finn sat six feet behind him, dark brown eyes touched with the milky light of the moon reflected off the rocks of the slope.

"I'll be hanged if you weren't worth the investment of that beef bone," the big man said.

Finn lifted his long, fine snout and barked.

———

S itting on the porch of his large house on the Crosshatch headquarters, Aidan Dempsey lifted the heavy stone mug of coffee liberally laced with Scotch whiskey to his mouth and sipped. The first pale light of dawn shone between the dark western peaks, and the birds were awakening.

He swallowed the potent brew then set the mug back down on the broad arm of his rocking chair. He tapped the fingers of his other hand on the chair's other arm. Not a patient man, he was even more impatient for his riders to return with that kill-crazy Dakotan riding belly down across his saddle.

Rage still burned in him as did indignation and exasperation.

How dare the man who'd murdered his son trespass on the Crosshatch headquarters. No one threatened Aidan Dempsey anywhere. Most certainly not here in his own home!

Suddenly his fingers stopped tapping the chair arm.

Dempsey pricked his ears, listening.

Hoof thuds sounded along the western trail.

They grew steadily louder until he could hear men talking. Agonized groans and grunts rose, as well.

Tack squawked and bridle chains jangled, and then a dozen riders rode into the Crosshatch yard, uncertain figures in the early dawn. A dozen riders, Dempsey thought, his heart quickening, burning. Twenty had ridden out of here several hours ago…

He pushed his heavy bulk, now clad in whipcord trousers, a cream shirt, and soft brown deerskin vest. His Peacemaker .45 was strapped around his waist. The Nordic had caught him unarmed. That wouldn't happen again. As he'd sat in his chair, holding his lonely vigil, he'd been touched with an annoying fear that the big man might circle around and enter the headquarters once more.

Might drill a bullet through the rancher's head.

The man had seemed grimly resolved to do so a few hours ago. Now, after Dempsey had sent men after him, that resolve might have grown into a deadly determination.

His fear now edging away, a building anger and

incredulity grew in the rancher as he walked across the porch to stand at the top of the steps, staring at the mounted men reining up before him. Two sat slouched forward in their saddles. One was his foreman, Creed Morgan, who held a hand over his left knee. Dark, oil-like blood oozed between his fingers, glistening in the first light of dawn. Another man a little farther back in the pack held an arm across his belly. His head was down, hat brim hiding his face. He was murmuring, voice quavering with agony.

"What in holy blazes?" Dempsey said, glaring at Morgan.

"Sorry, boss," the foreman said, wincing and shaking his head. "They had the high ground."

"'They?'"

"There was two of 'em." Again, the foreman cursed and clamped his hand down tighter on his knee. "I don't know who the other fella was, but they both could shoot—I'll give 'em that."

"You'll give 'em that, huh?"

Morgan jerked his bearded chin to glance over his shoulder. "Todd an' me—we both took bullets. We lost seven."

"You lost seven and then you turned tail an' ran."

"Boss, we had no choice. Live to fight another day. We'll get him. I promise you that. You know me. Last night just was not our night."

"Someone best fetch a sawbones, boss," said another man in the motley pack, glancing at the wounded man beside him. "Hanson took one in the guts."

"Go to hell," Dempsey said. "Stable your mounts and get into the bunkhouse. I'll be out in a minute."

As the men reined their mounts toward the stable, Dempsey glared at them, rage a brush fire inside him. He slid his .45 up and down in its holster, gripping the handles so tightly his knuckles were white.

CHAPTER SIXTEEN

Dempsey released his gun handle, snapped the keeper thong into position over the hammer, walked down the porch steps, and crossed the yard to the bunkhouse. The men having stabled their horses and gone into their lair, lamplight shone in the windows.

When he was thirty feet from the bunkhouse's front door, the door opened, and one of the men stepped out—a tough, wiry, little, former Indian fighter from Dakota. Rory McCready had a bony face with a long, hooked nose, heavy brow, and feral eyes. As he wheeled and headed for the stable, ostensibly to saddle a fresh horse, Dempsey said, "Where do you think you're going, McCready?"

The small man stopped and wheeled back to face his boss. In his low, typically hard, even voice, he said, "Creed wants me to send for the sawbones in Cimarron."

"Get back inside." Dempsey jerked his chin at the bunkhouse.

"Morgan said Hanson'll die without help."

"He'll die anyway."

McCready shrugged. "All right."

He moved back into the bunkhouse, Dempsey following. The rancher closed the door behind him and stood looking at what was left of his miserable crew sitting or lying on their bunks, smoking and passing a bottle. The gunshot Todd Hanson lay on a lower bunk twenty feet from the rancher. Hanson lay on his side, arms across his belly, knees drawn to his chest, writhing in misery. His hat was off, exposing the bald top of his head.

The foreman, Creed Morgan, lay on his own cot against the far wall, near the woodstove someone had laid a fire in. A coffeepot steamed and chugged. Morgan had his wounded knee raised and was wrapping a long scrap of a cut up bedsheet around it. He turned to McCready, and his cheeks turned red. His hat was hooked on the wall above him. His angular, bearded face glistened with pain sweat.

"What the hell are you doing back? You're supposed to be on the trail to town," he told the ex-Indian fighter from Belle Fourche.

McCready glanced at their boss but said nothing.

"You tinhorns don't deserve a sawbones." Dempsey walked toward his foreman. "When men fail me, they are not rewarded with medical care."

All heads in the room turned as though on the same swivel as the angry rancher stopped and stared down at his ailing foreman, who glared up at him. "You can't do that, you savage son of a bitch! The bullet's still in my leg, and can't you see Hanson's in a bad way over there?"

"Let me see your knee."

"What?"

"Let me see your knee."

The indignant foreman glared up at his boss, an incredulous cast to his dark eyes. Slowly, he pulled his hands away from the knee.

Dempsey glanced down at it. "Looks bad, all right."

"It is bad! That Nordic's a killer and no man to be hunted at night."

"Shut up, coward!"

"What?"

"I'll show you what cowards get from me." Dempsey pulled his .45.

Morgan stared up at him, wide-eyed. When the rancher raised the Peacemaker, menace in his eyes, the foreman's eyes widened even more, glinted in disbelief. He quickly reached for the .44 holstered on his right hip, but before he could get the six-gun even half drawn, Dempsey's revolver roared, smoke and flames stabbing from the barrel. The bullet took the foreman through his upper chest, his heart.

His eyes rolled back in their sockets, and he flopped back down on his cot, dead.

Dempsey wheeled and aimed the smoking Colt straight out from his right hip. The other men stared at him in hushed exasperation, sliding their gazes from the dead foreman to their boss. One man, a killer from southern Texas named Gabriel Armor, had a hand wrapped around the walnut grips of his Bisley .44.

Dempsey looked at him. "I'm gonna give you the benefit of the doubt and assume your hand went to your gun as an automatic reaction to gunfire."

Armor was leaning against the bunkhouse's far wall. He rolled a half-smoked, black cigar from one corner of his mouth to the other and blinked once. Then he removed his hand from the Bisley's grips. He said nothing.

Neither did the others.

Dempsey walked over to where the gut-wounded Hanson lay, no longer grunting but gazing warily at his boss from under a wool blanket. The man's eyes grew wider as the rancher approached his bunk.

In a voice pinched with pain, his eyes rheumy with agony, the man said, "Hoo…hold on…now…boss…"

Dempsey stopped at the foot of the man's cot. Still lying on his side, Hanson lifted his head from his pillow and stared at his employer in horror. He lifted one bloody hand out from under the blanket and held it palm out before him.

"Hold on, now, boss…"

"You know, Hanson," Dempsey said, raising the Peacemaker and ratcheting back the hammer, "I wouldn't let a gutshot dog suffer the way you're suffering."

The man's eyes and mouth opened wide as he slid his open hand farther out from his face. "Now, you hold—!"

Again, the Peacemaker roared. The .45-caliber bullet tore through Hanson's hand to plunk into his right cheek, just below his right eye. The man's bullet-torn hand dropped, his eyes closed, his head fell sideways against his pillow, and he expired with a single jerk and lay still.

Again, Dempsey wheeled to regard his men. Again, he held the Colt down by his right hip, aimed at the men regarding him darkly.

"Anyone wants to leave, leave now."

They looked at him, glanced at each other in silent conferral, then turned back to the rancher. No one said anything.

When after a full minute none of the men moved, Dempsey said, "Bury these two, have your breakfast, saddle fresh horses, and get after the Nordic. Don't come back until you bring him back…alive. I don't care if he's just a little alive. But I want him alive enough to recognize my face." He backed to the door, stopped, holstered the Colt, and said, "Now, I'm gonna go bury my boy."

He returned to the house, climbed the stairs to the second story.

He walked to the third door on the hall's right, twisted the knob, and opened the door. Lon lay in bed, propped on his elbows, staring at his father. He'd heard the shots in the bunkhouse, his father's heavy tread in the hall. The bandage on his nose fairly glowed in the room's misty shadows.

"Stop sulking. You're foreman now, God help us all. Get out there." Dempsey jerked his head to indicate the stable. "You'll be leading those men after the Nordic. Don't come back until you find him. Remember, I want a few breaths still in him."

Lon stared at him. His throat moved as he swallowed.

Dempsey drew his head back into the hall and closed the door.

———

I n the lemony light of midmorning, Nordic and Clara climbed the bench on the other side of which the line shack hunched, nicely concealed by the dense pines and firs around it, the ridge rising behind it.

They both checked their horses down when they saw Cimarron Town Marshal Bryce Adams saddling his horse tied to the hitchrack at the front of the cabin. He set his saddle atop the blanket he'd placed on the horse's back and then grabbed his bandaged right arm and swayed forward against the horse.

Finn sat beside Nordic, growling at the intruder.

"Easy, Finn."

The dog glanced up at the man and stopped growling, cocking his head from side to side, curious.

Nordic glanced at Clara then gigged Apache ahead at a gallop, reining in near the ailing marshal, who'd turned his head to regard him incredulously. Clara galloped her own mount ahead, as well, and reined up to Nordic's right, casting her own incredulous gaze at the big man on the Appaloosa.

"What the hell is he doing here?" she inquired, her tone brusque and disapproving.

Finn walked up and sniffed the man then backed away, apparently satisfied they'd met before, and he hadn't been a threat. The dog had probably known the lawman in town, as well.

"Easy, Clara," Nordic said.

"Easy this!" Clara reached forward and shucked her carbine from its saddle scabbard. She loudly jacked a round into the action.

Adams turned and leaned back against his horse, regarding Clara as though she were a mountain lion who'd just snuck up on him.

"Sheath it, Clara," Nordic said.

Clara kept the carbine aimed at the lawman. "How did he find you?"

"*He* found *me*," Adams said.

Clara glanced at Nordic in exasperation. "And you brought him *here*?"

"For some damn reason, I couldn't just leave him there to kick off alone."

"Let the man die. He knows where you are. He'll tell Dempsey and that popinjay English!"

"I won't," Adams said.

Clara kept the rifle aimed at the lawman, her gaze on Anders. "He's useless. And he's a coward. *Bad combination!*"

Adams chuckled and said, "Not even I would betray a man who saved my life."

Clara turned to him, frowning curiously. "What are you doing in the mountains?"

"My job, believe it or not." Adams looked at Nordic. "I reckon I just got confused about what that entailed, exactly." He slid his gaze back to Clara. "I'll do what I can to convince Dempsey and English that Dave Dempsey's killing was justified. Probably won't do any good, but…"

"Bullshit," Clara said. "You'll ride back to town, get good an' drunk, and tell them exactly where the cabin is. They'll ride up here, a whole horde of Dempsey's men, and burn Anders out. They'll probably burn Maggie's ranch because she helped him."

Adams slid his gaze back to Nordic. "I wish you'd just ride away."

"I wish I could."

Sitting beside him, Finn looked up at Nordic and whined, twitching his ears.

Anders said to Adams, "Your coming here got you into this as deep as me."

"Might be time to retire."

"You're in no shape to ride back to town."

"Believe it or not, I still have a job."

"You've lost a lot of blood."

Adams looked at his bandaged arm. The bandage was spotted with blood. He sighed.

Clara had let the rifle in her hands sag until it was no longer aimed at the lawman. Looking deeply puzzled, she slid her gaze from Nordic to the lawman and back again.

"If I didn't know better," she said, "I'd think you two had become friends."

Adams looked at Nordic and acquired a curious expression of his own. "I'm not sure what we are."

Nordic shrugged a shoulder. "There's nothing so complicated about it."

"Dempsey makes it complicated. He has a lot of men I can't do anything about. I'm going to call in U.S. marshals when I get back to town. I know the chief marshal in Albuquerque. We worked together back in the day. He'll send a passel of Federals to help me keep the peace."

"My god," Clara said in hushed astonishment to Adams. "What's got into you?"

The lawman gave a wan smile. "I must be drunk."

Anders knew the truth. The lawman knew what he'd become and didn't want to be that man anymore. It was as simple as that. Anders knew he could trust him. There'd never been many men he could trust.

"Well," Adams said, turning and grabbing his saddle horn, "I reckon I'd best be riding along. Burning daylight." Weakly, awkwardly, he toed a stirrup and swung heavily into the saddle, settling himself on the dapple gray, wincing at the pain in his arm.

He reined his mount around, touched heels to the horse's flanks, and lurched off in a trot, pinching his hat brim to Nordic and Clara as he rode past them.

Watching him go, Clara said, "Why is it I see a dead man riding?"

"Because he's tryin' to do the right thing. Poor bastard."

CHAPTER SEVENTEEN

An hour from the line shack, Adams halted the dapple gray.

His arm was burning. It felt like a branding iron was being held against it.

He looked at the bandage. More blood.

He'd been avoiding the whiskey. He didn't want to be that man anymore. He wasn't sure why. Maybe his life having been saved by Anders Nordic had taught him something about self-respect and doing what was right. By riding up to find the man's cabin, he hadn't been doing what was right. He'd been doing a powerful, corrupt man's bidding. The bidding of Aidan Dempsey and the just-as-corrupt banker, Reginald English.

He hadn't been following the law. He'd been following the orders of outlaws, for Nordic had had every right to shoot Adams's deputy, Dave Dempsey, in self-defense.

No, he didn't want to be that man anymore—a

corrupt lawman. He didn't want to be a drunk anymore, either. Still, his arm felt as though a red-hot railroad spike had been driven through it. He had to dull the pain, or he'd be in danger of passing out before he reached town, still another hour's ride away.

He reached back and fished his hide-wrapped bottle out of a saddlebag pouch.

He untied the leather string holding the hide in place, unwrapped the bottle, and pried out the cork. He sniffed the mouth, made a face. The Who-Hit-John smelled like horse water. He held the unlabeled bottle out away from him, staring at it. He shook his head.

"You're just gonna have to gut it out, Bryce. You've suddenly become mighty averse to drink. I'm thinkin' it's more what the hooch says about you than the smell. You've always known how it smells. Now it smells like a bad reputation. A corrupt soul."

He pulled the bottle back behind his left shoulder and threw it forward. It shattered on a large gray rock off the trail's left side.

He tossed away the hide and the string and gigged the mount forward, grunting through gritted teeth, "Time to gut it out. Time to gut the rest of your life out, you old sinner!"

He gigged his horse forward. He followed the trail through a copse of aspens and then into a broad clearing in a broad valley. On his left was a low, sage- and cedar-stippled ridge, like a long, low, natural bench. He glanced at it, turned his head back forward, then jerked his head back to his left, looking toward the ridge. He jerked abruptly back on his horse's reins, stopping the mount.

At least ten riders sat horses atop the bench, spread out roughly ten feet apart. They were all staring down toward Adams. A big man with a broad-brimmed, cream Stetson sitting a pinto in the middle of the pack had something white on his nose.

A bandage.

Lon Dempsey?

As Adams stared back at the riders staring down at him, Adams's heart thudded. They had a menacing air about them. Suddenly, he wished he hadn't been so hasty about discarding the whiskey. He could use a pull from it just now, to calm his nerves if not to ease the agony in his right arm.

This here looks like trouble. Lon Dempsey would have strayed from his home graze for no other reason than he was looking for Nordic.

Lon Dempsey turned his head to his right and then to his left, saying something to the others. Then he touched spurs to the pinto's flanks and moved forward, galloping down the bench toward Adams, the others following suit, spread out in a long line.

All right, don't panic, the lawman ordered himself. You're not that man anymore. You're the town marshal of Cimarron. Hell, you're Lon's boss…if he was still a deputy, that was. After his father had hauled him naked out of town in the back of a wagon, Adams was no longer sure what Lon was.

Maybe a wounded bear…

As the riders drew within fifty yards, apprehension

grew in Adams. He reached down and released the keeper thong from over the hammer of his holstered Colt. It was a timeworn, automatic response to possible trouble, from a time when he was younger and didn't mind courting it. He wasn't that man anymore, he was reminded by the fear building in him, seeing the hard set to Lon's jaw beneath his broken nose and swollen, purple eyes.

He'd been sent out by his father. Aidan Dempsey was not a man you lightly let down. Adams knew the man had a reputation for bull whipping men…even sons…who let him down.

The riders came at Adams so fast they frightened his gray. Adams kept a firm hand on the ribbons, but the dun whickered and sidestepped edgily.

Lon and the other riders drew up to within ten feet of the lawman and drew rein, curveting their mounts, dust sifting over the sage and short, blond summer grass behind them.

"Marshal," Lon said by way of grim greeting. "What brings you out here?"

"I was about to ask you the same thing," Adams said. "Kind of a long ways from home, Lon." The lawman glanced at the eleven men spread out in a semicircle around him, eyes set hard beneath the low-pulled brims of their weathered Stetsons. "Where's Morgan?"

"You know why we're out here," Lon said, dismissing Adams's second question.

Sensing the tension, the man's restive horse gave a loud whicker and blew. Lon kept his own firm hand on the reins. He canted his head to one side to look at Adams's bandaged arm. "What happened?"

"Rustlers."

"Ah," Lon said. "You'll find 'em out here if you find 'em anywhere. That's why Maggie Rae kept a man or two in line shacks all year round."

"That's the reason, all right."

"You seen him?"

"Who's that?"

Lon studied him, suspicion growing in his swollen, dark eyes. "You know who."

Adams glanced at the hard-faced men around him and sucked back the fear building in him. Shame grew along with his fear. He'd never used to be a fearful man. At one time, he'd been downright reckless. He figured age and drink had done it, then losing his family and marrying a young woman he didn't love but only wanted…felt he needed…for companionship in his later years.

All the while knowing he wouldn't be able to hold her, that eventually she'd find herself a younger man who didn't come with half of Adams's problems.

Adams said, "Go home, Lon. This is a job for the law, not vigilantes."

"I'm your deputy!" Lon said with a caustic grin.

"You know you're not out here for me. You're out here for your old man. To avenge Dave."

"Well, that's what we Dempseys do. We avenge one another."

"Hell, you didn't even ride out to retrieve his body."

Lon flushed. Anger of his own flashed in his dark eyes. "Where is he? I know you've seen him."

"Go home. This is a job for the law. I'm riding back to Cimarron. I'm going to send for U.S. marshals and an honest judge—not one of your father's flunkies —to settle this thing."

"The hell you are!" Lon scoffed. "Where is he?"

Adams didn't know where he got the spine to do what he did next—maybe out of a long-past habit and the rage and defiance building in him, knowing he was right and Aidan Dempsey was wrong, and he was tired of being the rancher's flunky. Maybe he was angry at himself, as well. For all the lost years. The lost pride.

Painful as the maneuver was to his wounded arm, he pulled his .44 from its holster with a swiftness that surprised even him. He held the revolver halfway out from his shoulder, sucking back the pain in that arm, and thumbed the hammer back. Narrow-eyed, he said, "Back off, you son of a bitch! I told you to go home, and you do it! Tell your father to stand down! I won't let him hang an innocent man. Those days are over."

Lon stared at his former boss in disbelief. Quietly, he said, "I'll be damned if you didn't pull iron on me. A Dempsey."

"You're no Dempsey. You're a dog afraid of disobeying its master. Go home, Lon." Adams hardened his jaws, felt hot blood rise in his cheeks. "Or take one in the guts."

In the corner of his right eye, Adams saw one of the other men close a gloved hand over the grips of his holstered six-shooter.

"Do it!" Adams bit out, twisting his mouth in rage. "I'd love to drill your boss one in the guts!"

The others looked at Lon, inquiringly.

Lon stared at Adams, his incredulous gaze sliding from the lawman's cocked Colt to his eyes, trying to read him.

"Leave 'em pouched, fellas," Lon said tightly, staring into the lawman's hard gaze.

"Rein around," Adams ordered. "Go home."

Lon kept his eyes on Adams's eyes. *He knows I'd do it*, Adams thought. *I don't know how he knows, but he knows. You can only tease a rattlesnake with a stick so long before it strikes.*

"All right," Lon said, keeping a firm hand on his jumpy mount's reins. "You won this round. We'll see who wins the next one." He reined the pinto around and yelled, "Come on, boys!"

He spurred the horse into an instant hard run. The other men cast their gimlet-eyed gazes at Adams and his cocked .44 once more, then reined their own mounts around and gigged them into hard runs after their boss. When the riders topped the bench and disappeared down the other side, Adams heaved a relieved sigh and holstered the .44.

His right hand trembled. His heart quivered.

He chuckled. "Where in the hell did *that* come from?"

He heeled his mount ahead and into a narrow, rocky canyon. He crossed an arroyo still wet from the previous night's rain and climbed the opposite bank. He'd ridden for another fifteen minutes when he stopped suddenly and turned his head to one side, listening.

The rataplan of galloping horses sounded behind him.

The hoof thuds grew steadily louder.

Adams looked behind him and saw Lon's crew galloping toward him, several just then shucking rifles from their saddle scabbards.

"Shit!" Adams said, turning forward and ramming his heels into his horse's flanks.

The gray whinnied, reared slightly, then took off at a dead run.

Adams crouched low in the saddle as the thunder of rifles rose behind him. He glanced over his shoulder and a stone dropped in his belly when he saw the Crosshatch riders gaining on him, Lon and his bandaged nose at the head of the pack, the others fanned out behind him in a wedge, smoke puffing from their rifles.

Bullets tore up sage and brush between the Crosshatch riders and Adams, some plunking into trees on each side of the trail. The gray took several more strides before a bullet carved a hot line along the left side of the lawman's head. Adams jerked forward in the saddle and lost his grip on the reins. Pain searing his skull, adding to the misery already caused by his wounded right arm, Adams clawed at the reins, but they dropped away.

As he slid down the galloping gray's left side, he flung his right hand at the saddle horn. His fingers brushed it and then he tumbled down his left stirrup, struck hard on the sage-peppered ground, and rolled, groaning, searing pain engulfing his whole being.

Before he came to a stop at the base of an aspen, he felt as though every bone in his body had been dislocated. Above his own agonized groans, he heard the approach of horses. He lifted his head to peer over his boot toes. The Crosshatch riders were within fifty yards and closing fast, dust rising behind them.

They drew rein ten feet from Adams.

Lon gigged his own horse forward and curveted him.

He stared down at the wounded lawman who lay like a turtle on his back. He reached for the Colt on his hip, but his holster was empty. He'd lost the gun in his tumble from his horse.

He looked from the empty sheath to Lon Dempsey staring down at him, eyes flat as a bear's eyes. Lon aimed his rifle at him and gave a death's-head grin.

CHAPTER EIGHTEEN

At the Flying W headquarters, Nordic and Clara reined up near where the dark, spidery Maggie Rae, clad in her customary denims and flannel work shirt, the sleeves rolled up her corded arms, was beating another rug to death on her wash line. A half-smoked quirley dangled from her thin lips, leaking ashes.

She was so intent on her job of pummeling the rug, grunting shrilly with every blow, making dust billow, that she'd neither seen nor heard her hired man and her niece ride up to the cabin.

Anders glanced at Clara then leaned forward against his saddle horn and cleared his throat, trying to gently announce his and Clara's presence so as not to startle the woman.

Maggie gave a witchlike screech of shock and horror and jumped back, dropping the stick and casting her deeply startled gaze at the newcomers sitting their saddles fifteen feet away from her. "Yeegads—you damn near skeered the life plumb out of my old, weary heart!" she shrilled.

"Sorry, Maggie," Anders said, straightening in his saddle and wincing. "I was afraid that would happen."

"You were afraid that would happen, were you?" Maggie said, pressing a hand to her bony chest and shuttling her gaze between her niece and Nordic. "Well, it did!"

"Sorry, Auntie," Clara said, sitting her bay to Anders's right.

Finn sat on the ground between them, studying the mannish-looking little woman curiously.

"And you," Maggie said, pinning her niece with her gaze. "Where on God's green earth have you been?" She returned her gaze to her hired man. "Well, I reckon it's obvious—ain't it?"

Clara glanced at Anders, flushing, giving an intimate little half smile.

She turned to her aunt. "I'm sorry I was gone so long. I didn't intend to be. Ran into a little trouble last night."

"You did, did you?" Maggie said. "I hope it didn't have anything to do with the gunfire I heard only a few minutes ago. Sounded like a pitched battle to the west!"

Again, Nordic and Clara shared a look.

Turning back to Maggie, Anders said, "Gunfire in the west? How far away?"

"Maybe a mile or two. It was distant but not *that* far away. I ran into the cabin and got my Henry down from the hooks above the door." She glanced at the rifle leaning against the cabin. "Just in case ol' Dempsey was gettin' notional again."

To Clara, Nordic said, "The main trail out of the mountains to Cimarron is over that way. Adams probably would have taken that route."

Clara frowned. "Think he ran into trouble?"

"Could be someone suspected he found me."

"Think he'd tell 'em? I know the Adams I once knew would."

Nordic shook his head resolutely. "No, I don't. Not now." He reined Apache hard right. "I'm gonna check it out!"

He booted the Appy into a gallop, heading west across the yard to the portal.

"Not without me, you're not!" Clara booted her own horse after him, turning her head to call over her shoulder, "Be back soon, Auntie!"

"Fool child!" Maggie cried, stomping one booted foot in frustration and anger. "You don't need to be ridin' into no lead swap, niece o' mine!"

Nordic and Clara couldn't push the horses too hard. They'd been on long rides, but at least the trip down from the cabin had been downhill instead of up, and both mounts naturally had a deep bottom. Because he knew Dempsey might have sent his men after them again, Anders had wanted to accompany Clara down to the Flying W's headquarters. Running and walking both mounts frequently, they still made good time, heading cross-country, following two creek-threaded canyons toward the main trail that connected the heart of the Chamas with Cimarron.

A half hour after they'd left the Flying W, Nordic lay belly down at the top of a ridge, studying the trail that ran along the ridge's opposite side through his spyglass. He saw nothing on the trail directly below him. He was about to lower the glass when he spied movement along the trail to the southeast, on his left.

They were a good ten riders heading generally in the direction of Nordic's line shack.

The man riding in the middle of the pack hipped around in his saddle to peer around him, and Nordic saw the bandage on the man's nose.

Apprehension rippled through Nordic like a chill breeze harassing a lake.

He lowered the glass and turned to Clara lying beside him. Finn lay between them, looking at Anders expectantly.

"What is it?" Clara said, eyes cast gravely.

"Pretty sure it's the Crosshatch men. Lon's leading them. Musta got a promotion."

Clara drew a deep, slow breath, keeping her dark gaze on Anders.

Nordic collapsed the spyglass and rose. "Let's check out the trail."

Clara and Finn rose, too, and Clara swung up onto her bay's back, gigging the mount after Anders who put Apache over the top of the slope and down the other side, Finn scampering behind them, tongue drooping over his lower jaw. At the bottom of the slope, Nordic turned Apache right, onto the trail, heading north toward town. He hadn't galloped far before he drew back sharply on the Appy's reins, his heart hammering his breastbone.

Something hung from a stout aspen branch off the trail's left side.

Clara checked her bay down beside Nordic. "What is it?"

Anders didn't say anything. He sat tensely, straight-backed, staring toward the object hanging from the aspen branch. However, what hung from the branch was no ordinary object.

It was a man.

Nordic put Apache on ahead, slowly. He didn't have to ride far, however, before there was no question about who, exactly, had been hanged from the aspen. A stout rope had been looped twice around Adams's neck, the rope thrown over the branch above him then tied off on a small spike branch near the base of the tree, on the opposite side of the aspen from where the town marshal hung, chin dipped to his chest, his slack body turning this way and that, the rope making soft creaking sounds beneath the rustling of the breeze in the leaves.

A bloody line ran along the left side of his head.

His short, sandy hair was still matted from his hat, which lay near his feet, which hung about four feet above the ground.

"Oh, for Chrissakes!" Anders said, staring up at the dead man in exasperation. It never ceased to astonish him what evil some men were capable of.

The lawman's eyes were half-open and seemed to be staring at his boots. His skin was already turning a waxy pale, though he likely hadn't been hanging here for long.

Finn sat between Nordic and Clara, staring at the dead man, shifting his weight from one front foot to the other, whining softly.

Clara turned to Anders. "Think they know where the cabin is now?"

"No," Anders said. "They're likely backtracking Adams, but if they find the cabin, nobody's home. They'll find me later or I'll find them." His jaws hardened. "Either way, they're all gonna die. Lon will go first."

Clara looked up at the dead lawman.

"They could have buried the body."

"Nah, they want it to be found. They want to pin the murder on me. Adams got too close to the cabin so I did what any savage Nordic would do."

"What are you going to do, Anders?" she asked, a note of dread in her voice.

Nordic swung down from his saddle and pulled his Green River knife. "I'm gonna cut Adams down and take him back to town."

"That's crazy! English and the whole rest of the town will think you did this!"

"They will, anyway. I want to be the one to report the hanging. Besides, Clara." Nordic looked at her as he dropped to one knee at the base of the aspen. "It's the right thing to do. I can't just leave him hanging here. He was going to help me. Now I'm going to help him one last time…see that he's treated properly. He told me he had a wife. She has to know."

Anders chopped through the rope just above where it was tied off at the base of the tree. He dropped the knife and grabbed the cut end with both hands. Straightening, he slowly paid out the rope, gently lowered the lawman's body to the ground, easing him onto his back, his head turning to one side, boot toes pointing straight up in the air.

Clara walked over to stand beside Nordic, who stood staring down at the dead man, Finn sitting beside him.

Nordic and Adams hadn't been friends long. But they'd been friends.

Clara shook her head, said softly, "I don't understand you, Nordic. You hate everyone yet you adopt stray dogs and you helped this man who wanted to arrest you at Dempsey's bidding."

Nordic just stared at Adams. Beneath his anger, he felt sick to his stomach.

Clara sidled up to him, rubbed her cheek affectionately against his shoulder. She smiled up at him.

Anders brushed his thumb affectionately across her chin.

———

Three miles from where he and the other riders had hanged Adams, Lon held up his right hand and drew rein, curveting his mount to regard the ten others. His horse blew, stomped a rear hoof, still unnerved by the sight of the dead man.

Lon was unnerved, as well. He'd known and liked

Adams at one time, though he had to admit he hadn't had much respect for him lately. But he'd found himself taken aback, after the fact, that he'd found himself capable of hanging him, his former boss who'd always treated him fairly. The truth was he'd done it because he knew it's what his father would have done. He had no doubt the old man would approve. Even admire the savagery Lon had found inside himself, the ability to do what needed to be done.

Adams had betrayed the Crosshatch. The way his father would have seen it, Adams had deserved the very punishment Lon had inflicted on him. Besides, he couldn't very well have let the man ride back to town and call the U.S. marshals in.

Now he said to the other riders, "Change of plans, fellas. You keep backtracking Adams. I'm gonna ride to town and report Adams's killing. I'm gonna tell English we seen that Nordic riding away from that tree like his hoss had tin cans tied to its tail."

"We can do that later," said a gray-mustached gunhand named Cole Gravy. "That just gives us more reason to hunt the man down and kill him! Then we can haul both bodies back to town an' this'll be over once an' for all!"

Anger rose in Lon. Anger and fear were a toxic mix, and he could feel both burning in his veins. "Don't question my orders, damn you, Cole! I'm the ramrod now. *Me!*" He thumbed himself in the chest. "I want the town to know Adams is dead and that the

Nordic did it. That'll steam them all up so no one will question our story."

He gestured with his arm.

"Now ride, dammit! You heard the old man! *Ride!*"

The ten glanced at each other dubiously then reined their horses around and continued along Adams's trail to the northeast, the direction of the Chamas's higher reaches.

When they were gone, anger still burning inside Lon, he cursed, reined his own horse back in the direction from which he'd come, and put the spurs to it, heading toward town where he'd report Adams's death but, more importantly, he could find a bottle and a woman.

Never before in his life had he needed his nerves calmed more than he did now.

Also—and he didn't really admit this to himself, at least not consciously—but the thought of going up against that big Norski again turned his spine to jelly.

CHAPTER NINETEEN

Reginald English looked especially small sitting in the high-backed, leather upholstered chair behind his nearly wagon-sized oak desk adorned with two matching lamps. The redheaded little man with the outlandish red mustache and side whiskers looked annoyed as he glanced up from the papers he was scribbling on with a carved wooden pen.

"What is it, Lon?" he asked with a sigh. "I'm very busy today. If you're not here to tell me you've run down the—"

Lon was walking into the banker's office, removing his battered Stetson. "Adams is dead."

English's lower jaw dropped. He set the pen down and sank back in his chair. "How?"

"Shot and hanged. Seems he caught up with the Nordic. Seen that bastard galloping away from the tree where Adams was hung."

"I...see...," the banker said with a sigh, entwining his beringed fingers together against his chest, steepling the two index ones. He stared down at them as though in prayer. "Don't doubt it a bit." He looked at Lon standing before his desk, his hat in his hands. "That savage."

Lon didn't say anything.

"Did you track him?"

"Me an' the boys were a long ways away. I seen him through my field glasses. We went after him but lost him. He's cagey. Lost his trail in some rocks, couldn't pick it up again. It's purty obvious to me he's used to being hunted."

"Yes, yes—of course he is."

"The boys are scouring the mountains for him. I rode to town, thought you should know. I sent the undertaker for the body. I couldn't find the marshal's hoss and mine was too tired for packin' a body down out of those mountains."

"Yes, yes. Homer will fetch him."

"If'n you want me to fill in for him...you know, before you can find another man for the job..." Lon patted his left front shirt pocket. "I took his badge."

English snorted subtly, causing ire to rise in Lon. "Thank you for the offer, but I have another man in mind."

"Who's that?" Lon couldn't keep his indignation out of his voice.

English gave his head a dismissive shake and leaned forward, placing his elbows on his desk. He looked down at his papers as though he were ready to get back to work. "Thanks for letting me know, Lon. I appreciate that."

He took up the pen, effectively dismissing the deputy.

Anger burning in him, causing heat to rise in his ears, Lon swung around, put his hat back on his head, and left the office, heels thudding loudly, spurs ringing. What did he expect? When a grown man is hauled out of town naked by his father in a box wagon, he'd be seen as a damn fool for the rest of his life…

He left the bank and stood outside on the boardwalk.

He was a writhing rattlesnake's nest of emotions.

Anger burned in him. So did his need for a drink and a woman.

He swung right and strode in the direction of Miss Aubrey's place.

———

Inside the Stockman's Bank of Cimarron, Reginald English rose from his desk, crossed the room, and poked his head out his door. He cleared his throat and said, "Charlie, a word with you, please?"

He closed the door and returned to the big chair behind his desk.

Presently, the door opened and a frumpy little, gray-haired man in a gray suit entered the office, holding a gray bowler in his hands. He was in his early sixties and had watery blue eyes. This was Charlie McMahon, English's "help," an all-encompassing title, in this case synonymous with "gopher."

"Yes, boss?" the man said in his customarily shy air.

"Fetch Gentleman Jim for me. He's renting a room at the Half-Moon."

McMahon nodded. "You got it, boss. Uh…"

Lines of annoyance cut across the banker's forehead. "Yes, yes—what is it?"

"Mind if I, uh…"

"Stop for a drink on your way back…?"

"Uh…yeah." McMahon ran the back of a shaky hand across his mouth. "Gettin' mighty dry…"

"Go ahead." English held up a finger. "But only one. Then I want you back here pronto. I'll have some letters I need you to run over to the post office."

"Thanks, boss." McMahon set his hat on his head and left the office.

———

L on pushed through the white, glass-paned door of Miss Aubrey's hurdy-gurdy house.

Miss Aubrey herself stood behind a small bar against the parlor's rear wall. It was flanked with several shelves teeming with shot glasses, beer schooners, and a dozen or so colorful bottles including labeled whiskey bottles. Lon drooled as he glanced at the shelves. A man could always get a good drink at Miss Aubrey's.

And a good woman, too.

It had taken courage for him to return here after being hazed out naked by his father. Such was the strong pull of the former schoolteacher's place, her hooch, and female flesh…

"Lon," Miss Aubrey said, clad in a colorful, revealing gown and holding her wooden cigarette holder.

She was just then filling two shot glasses. They were likely for the two men—ranch hands Lon vaguely recognized—parked on a green velveteen sofa against the room's far wall. They were sitting with two scantily clad girls with whom they were so deeply involved in conversation, the girls smiling and tittering, one running a finger through one of the hand's thin hair, that they didn't even look at Lon as he walked in.

As Lon approached the bar, Miss Aubrey set the shot glasses on a tray, and walked out from behind the bar. "I'll be right back."

She took the tray over to her only customers, set it down on a wooden table fronting the sofa, then strode back behind the bar, the skirt of her gown fluttering prettily around her long, slender legs. No wonder she'd had an affair with one of her students. Lon wouldn't mind having an "affair" with the pretty woman, either, but she'd long ago made it known she was strictly off-limits although rumors had it she was having an dalliance with a married businessman in town.

Lon slapped his hand on the bar. "Bottle. Scotch. And Miss Lilly."

"Uh…Lon," Miss Aubrey said, her lustrous brown eyes glinting in the light angling through the parlor house's front windows. "I think…I think…I can no longer allow the kind of trouble you too often bring to my establishment."

Lon scowled at her, the toxic wash of emotions roiling through him growing hotter, more toxic. "What?"

Miss Aubrey saw the anger in his eyes, the flush in his cheeks. She swallowed, set her hands palm down atop the bar, and spread her fingers. "I said…I can no longer—"

"Bottle," Lon said, his low voice pitched with menace.

Again, she swallowed. Her hands on the bar shook a little. "Lon…you're…hard on the girls…"

Lon reached into his shirt pocket and pulled out Adams's badge. He pinned it to his shirt and tapped it with his index finger. "I'm the law now. Adams is dead. I'm the law, Miss Aubrey." He held out his right hand, palm out. "Now, I'll take that bottle."

She looked at the badge on Lon's shirt. Her eyes shown with a growing apprehension. She lifted her hands from the bar, murmured, "All right." She grabbed a bottle off one of the shelves behind her, set it on the bar. Tonelessly, her heart withering with dread, she said, "You want the whole bottle, I take it…"

"Oh, yeah," Lon said, prying the cork from the bottle and taking a long pull. He pulled the bottle down and smacked his lips. "Been a long day."

"The marshal…he's uh…"

"Dead as a post." Lon chuckled, shook his head.

"That tree sure grew it some Adams fruit. It was the Nordic, sure enough. Mean as a grizzly." He chuckled again, took another pull from the bottle. Miss Aubrey stared across the bar at him. Behind Lon, the two ranch hands and the girls were still conversing in intimate tones, one of the girls occasionally crying out in sudden laughter then coyly covering her mouth.

"I'll be needin' Miss Lilly," Lon told the madam.

Aubrey drew a sharp, bracing breath and said crisply, "Miss Lilly is with another client."

Lon took another deep pull from the bottle, pulled it down, and said softly, "We'll see."

He swung around and headed for the stairs.

"Lon, no!" Miss Aubrey yelled, terror in her voice.

"Hey now," said a man's voice.

Lon stopped at the bottom of the stairs and glanced over his shoulder. The intimate chatter on the sofa had stopped. All eyes were on Lon. One of the cowboys stood in front of the couch. He was long, lean, and blond-haired, with a boyish face. He tried to look tough but there was fear in his pale blue eyes. He wasn't wearing a gun. Aubrey didn't allow guns in her place. She'd reluctantly yielded to Lon's because he was a deputy town marshal.

"Hey now, this," Lon said, unsheathing his Colt, aiming it straight out from his shoulder, and clicking the hammer back. "Sit down, you dull-witted cow nurse or I'll drill you a third eye."

The cowboy gulped, eyes widening.

Slowly, he sagged back down on the sofa. The

other three on the sofa stared at Lon as though he were a lion escaped from a circus.

Lon sheathed the Colt and started up the stairs, ignoring Miss Aubrey calling behind him, "Lon, you can't go up there. Lilly's with a special client! *Lon!*"

Lon heard her run to the bottom of the stairs just as he gained the second story and started walking down the short, dimly lit hall. There were four doors on each side of the hall. Loud grunting and groaning sounded behind the second door on the hall's right side. Lon tried the knob. The door was locked.

Lon stepped back, raised his right leg and thrust it forward, the bottom of his right boot smashing into it just below the knob. The door flew open, the latching bolt flying inside and landing on the wooden floor with a loud *ping*!

A girl screamed.

A man yelled.

The man was on top of the girl, Miss Lilly, on the room's small bed ahead and to Lon's right. The man raised his head to peer in wide-eyed horror over his left shoulder at the intruder in the doorway. A wing of salt-and-pepper hair hung down over one brow. He had a long, clean-shaven, angular face.

Lon threw his head back and laughed. "Why, Preacher McDougal!" He laughed again. "I *thought* I saw you sneakin' up the back stairs one night. Sure enough!" He clapped his hands and did a lunatic little dance in the open doorway. Then he looked at the Reverend Lawrence McDougal and the glee in his expression had been replaced with atavistic fury. "Get the hell out. She's mine!"

"No, Lon!" Lilly cried. She was a pretty little brunette, young but with all the right curves in all the right places which had never been more obvious than they were right now.

"You're mad!" the reverend shouted, scrambling off the girl and lurching, tall and lean as a fencepost, naked and pale, to the dark clothes neatly folded on a chair near the bed.

"Out!" Lon shouted. "Out! Out! Out!"

Hugging the clothes against his bony chest, the preacher ran past Lon and into the hall, heading for the rear stairs.

Lon closed the door, wedged a chair under the knob, securing it, then turned to the girl. She sat up in bed, leaning back against the headboard, holding a sheet up to cover her breasts. Her pale gray eyes were wide with trepidation.

"No…Lon…*please*…! You always hurt me!"

Lon laughed, set the Scotch bottle on a dresser, and unbuckled his cartridge belt, letting it drop to the floor.

"My turn," he said.

CHAPTER TWENTY

Nordic rode up out of an alley between a drugstore and a tonsorial parlor.

He reined to a stop between the mouth of the alley and Cimarron's main drag then drew back on Apache's reins, clucking to the mount, backing him a few feet deeper in the alley but not far enough that he could not see into the street and the Stockman's Bank of Cimarron sitting on the other side of it.

He'd just delivered Bryce Adams's body to the undertaker on a Cimarron side street. He'd managed to run down the man's horse and had led the body back to town wrapped in Adams's own bedroll strapped belly down across his saddle. Now he'd just spied none other than the man's cold-blooded killer and the lawman's former deputy, Lon Dempsey, step out of the bank to stand on the boardwalk fronting it.

Dempsey stood stock-still for a time as though pondering something.

He raised a hand to his mouth and, apparently

having made a decision, swung to his right and began walking south along the boardwalk on the west side of the street. Nordic gigged Apache out of the alley mouth, crossed the main drag, and joined the wagon and horseback traffic, slowly following Dempsey. Anders knew most of the people around him recognized him and knew what he'd been accused of. One or two might try to take a shot at him just to make a name for themselves. Let them try. They'd pay dearly for those bullets. He wasn't too worried about it, though. Most men were cowards, including Lon Dempsey.

Lon walked two blocks then entered a pink, two-story, clapboard parlor house with shingle hanging under the awning identifying the house as simply *MISS AUBREY'S*.

Nordic stopped Apache a half a block north of the parlor house that had the traditional red lantern blazing in a front window. Fury was a wild stallion inside him. He looked down to see that he had his right hand wrapped around the bone grips of his long-barreled .44.

Hold on, he warned himself. *Just hold on. You go in there with your gun blasting you're liable to get someone besides Lon Dempsey killed. Bullets go through bodies and walls, fer Chrissakes…*

He turned Apache down a side street to the west. He rode to the end of the street, to where the high, rocky desert began, then turned him back east, to the main drag. He'd thought reasonably through his options which wasn't something he normally did. He was too often a man enslaved by his passions, which was one reason he preferred to live alone in the tall and uncut, unperturbed.

Other men perturbed him.

He'd never been as perturbed, however, as Lon Dempsey had perturbed him.

He'd decided to wait until Dempsey left the hurdy-gurdy house to kill him.

However, when he came to the main drag, he swung Apache right, stopped him before Miss Aubrey's parlor house, swung down from the saddle, and tossed the reins over a hitchrack. It was as though he were under the influence of a malign hypnotist.

Jaws hard, heart burning in his chest, he mounted the boardwalk fronting the place, opened the door, and stepped inside. Immediately, he heard a girl screaming somewhere above. A pretty brunette in her early thirties and in a flowing, low-cut gown was just then stepping out from behind a short bar ahead of Anders and to his right, breaking open a sawed-off, double-barrel shotgun and sliding a wad into each tube. As she did, she walked toward a staircase.

Nordic crossed the room, nudged the shotgun out of the pretty woman's hands.

"I'll take it from here," he said, and mounted the stairs.

On the second floor, he stopped at the door behind which the girl was screaming in agony. Lon was grunting savagely. Bedsprings were whining. Nordic kicked open the door, knocking a chair wide, and stepped into the room, his cocked Colt aimed straight out before him.

Lon looked at him over his shoulder, widened his swollen eyes to either side of the white bandage on his nose. His lower jaw sagged in shock.

The girl stopped screaming and looked at Nordic over Lon's right shoulder.

Nordic wagged the gun. "Off her."

Lon stared at him, terror in his eyes.

Nordic's own eyes bored into Lon's.

Lon jerked suddenly and climbed off the bed. He stood facing Nordic, hands raised high above his head.

"No," he muttered. "Please…don't kill me."

"You killed Adams."

"No! I mean…"

"I know what you mean. Here's what I mean," Nordic said. "Prepare to shake hands with the devil you low-down, dirty, ugly, sniveling sonofabitch."

"You can't kill me! I'm a Demp—!"

Anders shot him three times in the chest.

Lon flew back through the window behind him and landed with a thud in the street below.

Nordic holstered his .44, walked downstairs, pinched his hat brim to the pretty young madam standing at the bottom of the stairs staring at him incredulously. As he strode past her, heading for the front door, she said, "Did you kill Adams?"

"I just killed the man who killed Adams."

Nordic went outside, mounted Apache, and rode to the southeast end of town where Finn sat waiting for him off the trail's right side. As they'd approached

Cimarron earlier, Finn had slowed his pace and whined. The dog had been reluctant to return to the town that had mistreated him so badly. Nordic had told him he could wait at the edge of town for him. That's what he'd done.

"Come on, Finn," Anders said now, trotting Apache along the trail. "Let's head back to the tall an' uncut!"

Finn barked and ran along beside him.

Nordic laughed.

Cut from the same cloth, he and the dog were.

———

In the Stockman's Bank of Cimmaron, a soft double knock sounded on Reginald English's office door.

"Come," English said.

The door opened and a tall, thin man in a black hat, black duster over a black brocade coat, and a burgundy foulard tie entered the office. He was pale with a long face. A long, black cigar drooped from one corner of his broad, thin-lipped mouth. He exhaled smoke and blinked his pale lids with long, black lashes slowly as he closed the door behind him. He moved with a raptor-like fluidity. His dark, wide-set eyes also owned the air of a hawk or an eagle.

"You wanted to see me?" he said, as he folded slowly into the Windsor chair set against the wall beside the door.

He crossed his long, thin legs and rested a sheathed rifle across his thighs.

His thick mustache looked black as a raven's wing set against his pasty pale, broad-cheeked face. Long black sideburns slid down from beneath his hat.

"Are you free for the next week or so?"

"Gentleman" Jim Ridgely, a regulator so formidable no lawman would tangle with him, not even U.S. marshals, was often employed by area ranchers or prominent businessmen, including English, who wanted competitors or particularly slippery rustlers kicked out with a cold shovel, so to speak. Only, Ridgely employed his Sharps Big Fifty which he took with him everywhere and which he was so handy with he could shoot a moving figure from three hundred yards away.

"I'm not currently employed, if that's what you mean," the killer said in his heavy English accent. "More's the pity."

"Now you are," English said.

———

An hour later, Nordic and Finn passed under the wooden crossbar of the Flying W portal and trotted into the yard. It was late afternoon, and the shadows of the buildings including the log cabin on the other side of the yard from the small bunkhouse stretched long over the yard's hard-packed dirt and finely ground straw and horse manure.

Nordic saw no one about the place and began to

grow concerned until the cabin's halved-log front door opened and Maggie Rae stepped out onto the porch, wielding her Henry. She raised it in both hands, a hard, angry expression on her deeply tanned and lined features, black hair customarily drawn taut into a bun atop her head.

"Who in the hell...?" When her gaze found Anders, Maggie raised her brows and lowered the repeater. "Ahh...it's you. The man who has my niece mooning around here like a girl half her age. Can't even keep her mind on smoking a roast, let alone cleaning out a pantry!"

It was then that Nordic smelled the savory aroma of meat being smoked and saw blue-gray smoke rising above the house's far end. That was where Maggie and Clara had a small wooden smoke shack with a tin pipe rising from the roof. Just then Clara appeared, walking out from that end of the house, a wooden bowl and a basting brush in her arms. Her long, brown hair was drawn up in the style of her aunt's and secured in a bun atop her head, though not as tightly as Maggie's. Her pretty cheeks were flushed, and she cast an annoyed look at her aunt holding the rifle atop the porch.

"Oh, Aunt Maggie, how you do go on!"

"Hah!" Maggie screeched, delighted with herself. "You're supposed to be basting that beef haunch."

"I did!" Clara walked up to stand before Nordic and Apache. Finn gave a happy bark and ran up to the girl, turning to face Anders and rubbing his large, shaggy body up against Clara's leg, wanting to be petted by the young woman he'd befriended every bit as much as he'd befriended the big, bearded Dakotan. To Anders, she said, "How did it go in town?"

"I killed Lon."

"In *town*?"

"Looked like he'd talked to the banker. Was spreading the lie it was me who killed Adams."

"That low-down sonofabitch!"

Sitting beside Clara, Finn barked.

"Yep." Anders looked at Maggie. "Everything all right here?"

"So far, so good. Heard you culled Dempsey's herd a mite."

"A mite. They're still looking for me. After Lon's visit to the bank, I'm thinkin' English might sign up more men for the hunt. I have a feelin' when that little tinhorn gets a mad on, it's hard to take it off."

"Oh, it is. It is," Maggie said. "I know Reginald English. You don't want to cross him or miss a mortgage payment."

"Don't doubt it a bit."

"Stay for supper?" Clara asked.

Anders glanced at the sun's angle through one narrowed eye. "Think I'll push on home. Been a long day. Ol' Angus needs oats an' water and let out to graze around the cabin for a while."

Clara pulled her mouth corners down in disappointment.

"Clara, you go tend that roast," Maggie ordered.

Clara scowled at her aunt. "I just tended it!"

"Tend it again! You're not so big I can't still bend you over my knee!"

Clara glanced at Nordic, rolled her eyes, patted Finn, then wheeled and strode back around the far end of the cabin.

When she was gone, Maggie leveled a hard gaze on Anders. "You have her heart, you know?"

"I know."

Maggie pointed an admonishing finger at him. "Don't you let her get any fool notions in her head!"

"She won't."

"She loves you. Do you love her?"

"Yes."

Maggie pursed her lips and shook her head.

"She's no fool," Nordic said. "You know that, Maggie."

He pinched his hat brim to the woman, neck-reined Apache, turning the horse away from the porch, and put him into a trot around the cabin's near end, past the wash line, crossing the yard, pushing through brush, splashing across a narrow creek, and climbing a pine-clad ridge, heading south.

————

Behind him, Clara stood with her back against the end of the cabin, near where the smokehouse hunched in the brush and pines. She stood near the corner from where she'd overheard her aunt's and Anders's conversation.

Tears streaked her cheeks.

———

As usual, and just like he and Clara had done on their way into the mountains from town, he traced a circuitous route over hard ground, obscuring his trail so it would be hard even for an expert tracker to follow.

He'd ridden maybe only fifteen minutes when rifles barked behind him, back in the direction of the Flying W. Men shouted and a woman screamed.

Clara!

Instantly, Nordic stopped, heart pounding, then reined the Appaloosa around and galloped back the way he'd come, Finn following close on Apache's heels. When he drew within a hundred yards of the Flying W headquarters, a cold snake writhed in Nordic's belly. A handful of riders sat horses in the middle of the yard. Two were unmounted. Three men lay unmoving in the brush between the small bunkhouse and corral—Maggie and Clara's elderly hands, no doubt. They hadn't had a chance. Two of Aidan Dempsey's men—who else could they be?— were on foot while two mounted men held the reins of the dismounted men's horses. They had Maggie and Clara lying on their backs in the yard, each man with a foot on their chests, holding them flat. They aimed rifles at each woman's head, taunting them. Maggie was yelling, writhing, and cursing at the duster-clad Crosshatch man holding her down, the maw of his Winchester only inches from her forehead.

Nordic booted Apache into a ground-pummeling

gallop, hearing beneath the thudding of the horse's hooves the man holding Clara down, saying, "We're gonna kill that dried-up old hen but you…we're gonna have a *real good time* with you, pretty girl! Then you're gonna tell us where the Nordic is!"

He kicked Clara onto her belly then dropped to his knees, set his rifle down beside him, and proceeded to pull her trousers down, exposing her pale rump.

The other men laughed and swung down from their saddles to partake of the festivities.

Maggie shouted up at the man holding her down. "You go to hell you ten-cent bastard son of a Deadwood whore!"

The man laughed. His Winchester barked. Maggie stiffened then went slack, bright red blood oozing from the hole in her forehead.

"*NOOO!*" Nordic bellowed, galloping to within fifty yards of the killers from the Crosshatch now and going to work with both his Winchester and Colt, head down, his reins in his teeth.

Behind him, Finn barked furiously.

Anders's first shot drilled the man who'd just shot Maggie through his right ear, sending him sprawling. The horses of the other men spread out and galloped off, whinnying shrilly, giving Nordic an open path to their dismounted riders. The Crosshatch killers swung toward the man galloping toward them in mad fury, raising their Winchesters.

None got off a single shot before Nordic's hornet-like swarm of hot lead cut them down and sent them screaming off to their bloody demises.

CHAPTER TWENTY-ONE

The next morning, just after dawn, Aidan Dempsey stepped out of his ranch house with a steaming mug of coffee in his hand.

He walked to the top of the broad steps and turned his gaze to the bunkhouse.

He frowned.

No lamplight shown in the bunkhouse windows. That would have been odd on any other morning. Maybe not so odd on this particular morning. The few men he had left were likely still out scouring the mountains for the major thorn in Dempsey's side.

The Nordic.

The rancher lifted his stone mug to sip his coffee but then lowered it and switched his gaze to the wooden ranch portal and the mouth of the trail leading out of the yard. From a distance he heard the hooves of galloping horses and the rattle of a wagon. The sounds grew louder until four horseback riders flanked by a buckboard wagon emerged from an aspen thicket.

Apprehension rippled down Dempsey's spine. He and his daughter and wife were alone here. He didn't have a man on the place. Not even a cook. He'd fired the last one a month ago for drunkenness and general sloth. He considered fetching his rifle but then, as the riders passed under the portal and entered the yard, he saw the lead rider's ridiculously large, red mustache beneath the brim of his crisp, brown bowler.

He moved down off the steps as the four riders led by Reginald English climbed the slope and approached the house, the buckboard behind them. "Good Lord, English," the rancher said above the buckboard's clatter, "I thought you kept banker's hours. What're you doing out this early?"

The buckboard stopped behind the banker and the other riders—men Dempsey recognized as three tough nuts and saloon flies from town. English stared down from the back of his fine Morgan, trouble in his gaze.

"What is it?" the rancher asked him. "Trouble?"

"I'm afraid so, Aidan."

"What is it now?"

English sighed, stretched his furry upper lip back from his teeth. "Aidan, if you have anything stronger than coffee in that cup, you'd better take a sip. You've lost another son."

Dempsey felt a hitch in his heart. Dread pooled with the coffee in his belly. "You can't mean Lon. He's out with my men. They're scouring the mountains for the Nordic."

English shook his head darkly. "He came to town yesterday afternoon."

Incredulity and a building fury carved deep lines across Dempsey's ruddy forehead. "I gave him strict orders to…"

"He was in town. At Miss Aubrey's place. That's where the Nordic shot him."

The rancher had to consciously plant his feet to keep from stumbling backward and falling against the porch steps. He just stared up at the banker, his tongue a chunk of dry rawhide in his mouth.

The rancher tossed a look at the buckboard behind him. Another tough nut from town sat on the driver's seat.

"He's in the wagon," English said.

Dempsey swallowed. He turned to set his cup on the steps then moved stiffly to the wagon. He peered over the side panel to see a simple wooden coffin in the bed. He looked at the driver and, his heart pounding with dread, raked out, "Remove the lid."

The driver sighed. "If you say so, Mr. Dempsey."

"I say so. Open it."

The driver stepped over the seat and into the wagon's bed. He lifted the lid from the coffin. As he did, English moved up to stand beside the rancher. Dempsey stared down into the coffin at his dead son staring up at him from each side of his bandaged nose. Lon's mouth was open. He seemed to express shock in his swollen eyes.

Fury burned in the rancher's belly. His mind was a mix of questions and emotions. What had Lon been doing in town? What had the Nordic been doing in town? How had they come together?

The questions were vague, only half formed. He didn't know how to express them.

"I'm sorry, Aidan," English said, softly.

Then words oozed up from deep in the rancher's throat. "How in holy hob did…?"

He let his voice trail off when the thudding of yet more distant hooves reached his ears. He turned to stare at the trail once more, as did English and the other four mounted men as well as the driver still holding the lid of Lon's coffin.

"If that's my men," Dempsey said, "they sure as hell better have the Nordic with him." He punched the top of the side panel with the end of his fist. "I want to kill him myself. Hang the son of a…"

Yet again his sentence trailed off unfinished. Seven horses were just now passing under the Crosshatch portal. He'd expected to see men riding upright in their saddles. That was not the case, however, the rancher now saw to his own horror. All seven riders lay belly down across their saddles, legs and arms hanging stiffly. They were tied wrists to ankles beneath their horses' bellies.

"Good god!" English said.

Dempsey turned away from the wagon and started walking down the hill to the yard where all seven horses stopped near the corral gate, the mounts inside the corral coming up to the fence to greet them incredulously, sniffing the air cautiously, anxiously. Horses did not like the smell of dead men.

English walked just behind the rancher, the three

riders from town following on their horses. No one said anything.

Dempsey stopped fifteen feet from the mounts and their grisly cargo. He didn't need to go any closer. He recognized the men, though he could see only the backs of their heads, the colors of their shirts. He recognized Ringo Walsh by the large ring he wore on his little finger like a gentleman, though he was known for his uncouth behavior and cold steel skills.

Had been known, rather.

Obviously, those skills hadn't been good enough.

"That's the last of my men," Dempsey said under his breath.

He turned his dreadful gaze back to the trail. Out there, somewhere, lurked that big, blond-headed killer from Dakota.

English patted Dempsey's shoulder. "Don't worry, Aidan. I've taken care of it."

Dempsey turned to him, arching an incredulous brow.

———

Nordic set a last rock on one of the four graves he and Clara had spent the night digging. The four graves formed an arrowhead of sorts, Maggie Rae's at the head of the others belonging to her three older hands who'd been cut down by Dempsey's men as they had run out of the bunkhouse after Maggie, according to Clara, had been shot down when she'd been heading for the well for water.

Bushwhacked.

Clara, making supper inside the cabin, had run out to see to Maggie when the seven Crosshatch men had stormed the yard, whooping, hollering, and shooting like a pack of rampaging Indians, and ridden Clara down and shot the three old hands as they'd run out of the bunkhouse, returning fire.

Anders walked over to where Clara stood over her aunt's grave fronted by a cross which she had fashioned from two dead branches and rawhide. Finn sat nearby in respectful silence, looking up at the grief-stricken young woman, his brown eyes doughy with deference and understanding.

Nordic doffed his hat and stood beside her, gazing regretfully down at the freshly mounded rocks.

"Those bastards," Clara said, slowly shaking her head. "They just wouldn't let it go."

"No," Anders said, guilt raking him.

Clara was staring down at her aunt's grave because of him. There was no mistake.

She looked up at him. "I never felt more satisfied than when you galloped in and cut them all down before they could get off a shot."

"There are two more," Nordic said, quietly.

Clara returned her gaze to the grave. "Yes."

"Not for long," he added, again quietly but with his voice drawn taut.

Again, Clara looked up at him then nodded and stared down at the grave again.

Finn whined and shifted his weight from one front paw to the other. He gave a single, resolute bark, gazing up at the man who'd rescued him from a hellish life in town.

There were two men still alive who shouldn't be, Anders thought. Dempsey and the banker, English. Nordic still had two jobs to do. When those were done, he'd leave here. He knew he wasn't responsible for all the hob that had been raised here. He'd only saved a dog. The actual killers were responsible. But it was time for him to leave, to let Clara get back to her quiet life here at the Flying W. He didn't want to leave her. He loved her. A strange feeling for him. An alien one. But it was time to leave.

But for now…

"Let's saddle up and ride to the line shack," he said now. "You'll have to stay with me and Finn until I've finished cleaning up this mess."

"I'll stay here…with Maggie," Clara said, flaring her nostrils angrily.

Anders shook his head. "Not a chance. Dempsey will hire…"

Distantly, a horse whinnied. Tied to a pine branch nearby, the unsaddled Apache returned the whinny, switching his tail. In the golden light of midmorning, Nordic saw six horseback riders on a knoll west of the ranchstead, to the left of the main trail that led out of the mountains to Cimarron. They were staring down into the Flying W headquarters.

One of the lead riders sitting his cream stallion slightly ahead of four of the others was a big and bulky man wearing a high-crowned brown Stetson. Snow-white muttonchops ran down along the sides of his broad, red face. The other man, sitting a black Morgan beside the big man, was small and impeccably dressed in a three-piece suit. An outlandish red mustache mantled his upper lip.

Rage burned in Anders.

Heart thudding heavily, he walked over and picked up his Winchester from where it leaned against a ponderosa pine. He raised the rifle and angrily pumped a cartridge into the action, staring back at the riders with barely bridled fury, threateningly…challengingly, letting the rancher and the banker know he was ready to send more men back to the Crosshatch riding belly down across their saddles.

The two lead riders neck-reined their horses around and galloped down the backside of the knoll, gone. The others followed.

Finn turned to Nordic and moaned inquiringly.

Clara stood staring at the now-vacant hill. "What're they doing here?"

"Visiting the scene of their crime."

And wondering where Dempsey's dead men had come from. They'd backtracked the horses that had carried them to the Crosshatch, dead. Now, the two men knew.

Still staring at the knoll, Clara said, "Are you going after them?"

Nordic shook his head. "All in good time."

Finn gave a single approving bark.

"We'd best saddle up, honey."

"I just have to say goodbye one last time."

Clara had picked a handful of mountain wildflow-

ers. Now she dropped to a knee and set them gently on
the rocks covering Maggie's grave. She left her hand
on the flowers, sniffed back a sob and said, "Goodbye,
Auntie. I love you and miss you already, hearing your
cackling laugh, smelling your venison stew, hearing
you humming in the early morning while you knocked
pots and pans together, whipping up pancakes or
griddle cakes…"

She sobbed again and covered her mouth with her
forearm. Her shoulders quivered with emotion. Finally,
she lowered her arm, drew a deep, ragged breath, and
rose, the morning breeze jostling her hair, kissed by
the golden sun as it sifted through the aspen branches
and pine boughs. It sounded appropriately solemn and
mournful, Anders thought.

Nordic saddled Apache then he and Clara rode
double down into the yard and over to the stable. In
the corral, Clara roped her bay, opened the gate, turned
the six other horses loose, for there would be no one
here to tend them for a while. When the horses had
galloped off, a few kicking their rear legs and shaking
their heads dubiously, Clara let her cat out of the
cabin. Thomas Aquinas would have to fend for himself
for a while, which he was fully capable of doing. She
gave the purring cat a parting kiss then mounted up.
She and Anders rode around the now-vacant house to
the south, climbing the southern ridge through the
forest rising above the Flying W cemetery and its
latest residents.

Clara gave another sob but did not look back.

Nordic and the bereaved young woman traced an

altogether different route than any of the other ones they'd taken either down from or up to the line shack, wanting to leave no well-worn trail. Still, they'd ridden only twenty minutes or so, rising steadily above the Flying W headquarters, when Anders felt goose bumps rise along his spine.

A surefire sign they were being followed.

He and Clara had just crested a ridge and started down the opposite side. Now he reined up, and said, "Wait here," and swung down from his saddle. "Stay with Clara, Finn."

He dug his spyglass out of his saddlebags, unpouched it, and tramped up to the crest of the ridge before lying belly down, doffing his hat, and gazing through the glass back the way he and Clara had come.

He whistled under his breath.

"More cannon fodder," he said.

CHAPTER TWENTY-TWO

F our horseback riders rode through aspens peppering the canyon through which Nordic and Clara had ridden only minutes before.

Nordic suspected they were the four men who'd been riding with Dempsey and English. Dempsey and English probably sent them on to track Nordic while the rancher and banker headed back to the Crosshatch for brandies and cigars on Dempsey's broad porch, soothing their nerves. Especially Dempsey. The man's entire bunkhouse had been wiped out and turned toe down. Nordic assumed the four men riding with them now English had hired out of some saloon.

Ne'er-do-wells. Not real cowhand material, but they'd do in a pinch.

The four men rode spread out unevenly, sporadically leaning out from their saddles, following Nordic and Clara's trail. As always, he'd ridden in such a way as to leave little sign. They'd probably followed him and Clara out of the Flying W yard, staying close enough to keep an eye on them. The breeze had blown from the southwest, roughly the direction Anders and Clara were riding. That's why neither horse nor Finn had winded them.

Nordic collapsed his spyglass, crawled a few feet down the ridge, doffed his hat, rose, and tramped back down to where Clara stood holding the reins of both their horses. She regarded him incredulously.

"Dempsey and English?"

Nordic dropped the glass back into his saddlebags. "I think they lost their stomach for the fight. They sent the four who were with them at the Flying W. Amateurs." He took his reins from Clara. "You keep riding. Follow Willow Creek. Take Finn with you." He turned to the dog. "Boy, you stay with Clara." He canted his head toward the young woman.

Finn gave an acknowledging yip and looked at Clara, ears standing.

"All right," Clara said. "I know I don't need to remind you to be careful."

Nordic smiled at her and swung up onto Apache's back.

When Clara galloped off down the ridge, Finn following closely behind but glancing over his shoulder to regard his regular companion, Nordic rode off across the shoulder of the ridge, straight south. He rode down the end of the ridge to Willow Creek and followed the creek, which ran through a shallow canyon, back in the direction he and Clara had come, generally back toward where the four riders were following him. He followed the creek, thickly sheathed in pines and aspens, back north to where he figured he'd likely intercept the four riders and show them the error of their ways.

He waited in the trees near where he and Clara had ridden, expecting to spy the four men soon.

He did not.

All he saw on his and Clara's back trail were sun-dappled, breeze-jostled aspen branches.

Cursing, he booted Apache out of the trees and rode back to the northeast, scouring the ground. He'd ridden five minutes before he saw a branch recently snapped off an evergreen shrub to his right. Just beyond the shrub, farther right, he saw half of a recent hoofprint.

He cursed sharply under his breath and whipped Apache to the northwest, toward the ridge from which he'd glassed the four riders. Maybe, like a tinhorn, he'd allowed the sun to flash off the lens of his spyglass, and they'd figured, knowing his reputation, that he'd come for them. Having guessed which direction he'd come from, they were trying to ride around him. He crested the ridge and galloped down the opposite side, desperate to reach Clara before they ambushed her.

At the bottom of the ridge, he swerved to the right, following a long, deep curve along Willow Creek over which he splashed and then galloped along the creek's south side, the creek now on his left. It curved along the base of a high, pine-carpeted ridge. A quarter mile beyond, the ridge fell away and he was riding along the creek through a piney flat. He hadn't ridden much farther before a rifle barked ahead of him.

Again, he cursed, heart thudding, and booted Apache into an even faster run.

They got to her. They'd outsmarted him and got to her!

Another rifle shot resounded. A few seconds later, another one rocketed around the forest.

Nordic followed another bend in the creek to his left.

Reins dangling and bouncing along beside her, Clara's bay galloped toward him, wide-eyed, ears laid back. The horse whinnied then galloped past Nordic and Apache, shaking its head. Badly scared.

Anders had just imagined Clara lying along the trail where she'd been blown out of her saddle, and his ribs turned to ice. But then he saw her ahead, hunkered down behind a rock along the side of the creek, just then racking another round into her carbine, shouldering the rifle, and firing across the creek and into the forest beyond. Finn lay on the ground beside her, panting and gazing across the creek into the woods into which she was shooting.

Nordic reined Apache to a skidding halt, shucking his Yellowboy, leaping out of the saddle then turning the horse and slapping his rump with a sharp *crack!* sending Apache galloping after Clara's bay, out of harm's way. Crouched low, he ran over and dropped to a knee to Clara's left, saying, "Thank God. I thought you—"

Clara ejected her last spent cartridge, jaws hard,

and said, "I don't see them now, but I saw them a few minutes ago, trying to ride up around me."

Nordic slid the shrubs before him apart, so he had a clearer view into the woods. He saw nothing but pines and aspens and sun-dappled forest duff. He kept surveying that side of the creek. Then he saw brief movement atop a low rise maybe fifty yards away.

"Did you see him?" Clara said.

"I saw. They're trying to get around us, cut us off."

"And shoot us out of our saddles," Clara spat out.

"Glad you saw 'em."

"I saw all four. They were close enough that I recognized Grady Holmes. Used to be a deputy sheriff till he got caught cattle rustling. Now he's a petty thug and horse thief. I have a feelin' the other three are his partners Bill Black, Charlie Winston, and Deuce McGill. They all came out to the Flying W last year lookin' for work. Maggie wouldn't hire them because she suspected…and so did I…they were wanting jobs on Flying W graze so they could rustle us blind."

"That was why it was so easy for Dempsey and English to hire 'em."

"How I figure it."

Nordic looked out across the creek once more. He spied no movement save the leaves and branches. He scanned the forest on the other side of the creek for a good minute before he turned to Clara and said, "Let's fetch our horses, keep riding."

"They'll dog us straight to the line shack!"

Anders grinned. "No, they won't. Let's go. Come on, Finn!"

Finn yipped and gained his feet.

Nordic rose, pulled Clara to her feet then, shepherding her along ahead of him and walking quickly backward, staring out across the creek from where bullets could come, retraced their route back down their trail. Finn ran ahead with Clara. When he was a good sixty yards from where he'd found Clara hunkered behind the rock, Anders turned forward and jogged with her and Finn around the broad bend in the creek.

They found the horses ten minutes later, grazing idly on the high, green grass growing along the creek bank. Both saddles had come loose. Nordic and Clara tightened the cinches, slid their rifles into their scabbards, and mounted up.

Clara pulled her hat brim low on her forehead and turned to her trail partner.

"Which way?"

Anders peered straight south, toward where a large rocky formation rose, misty with distance, a mile or so away, in higher, more broken country than that which they were in now. He tossed his chin.

He booted Apache into a trot, cutting through a side canyon. He booted the mount into a lope as they climbed the steadily rising terrain into an area of rocky dikes and escarpments. Finn ran along beside him, panting anxiously, instinctively knowing trouble was afoot. The Norski from Dakota traced a twisting course through country he'd investigated while checking on Maggie's herd, the high formation growing before them.

"If you're not careful," Clara said, "you're gonna lead us into a box canyon."

"That's the idea."

Ten minutes later, he swung to the right between two high ridges and followed the trail into a bottleneck formation at the base of the ridge he'd been aiming for. The trail led to the apron base of the ridge up which they climbed until they came to a long, shallow cave around which wild berry bushes and a few cedars grew. Rocks of all sizes littered the slope up which they'd climbed to gain the cave.

Finn lowered his head to peer into the cavern, his nose working as he sniffed, investigating the cave with his tail arched.

"How did you know about this place?" Clara asked, regarding Nordic incredulously. "Nobody knows about this place. Not even me, an' that's sayin' something!"

Nordic chuckled. He and Apache had scoured these mountains for fun as well as for work, hazing cattle by ones and twos back out onto the main range so they wouldn't be forever lost. He'd spent a night here eating a rabbit he'd shot, roasted on a stick, and washed down with hot, black coffee. The stars had been low, bright, and pointed.

While cool, it had been a good night. Solitude had wrapped itself around him like a warm blanket. He'd enjoyed that feeling of being alone from a very early age.

He swung down from Apache's back and led the

horse along the base of the formation, to the right of the cave. "Follow me."

Clara sighed, swung down from her saddle, and led her bay behind Nordic and the Appaloosa. A notch appeared in the wall ahead of Nordic. Not just a notch but a long, gravel-floored corridor leading back into the formation.

"My god," Clara said in a voice hushed with awe. "What *is* this?"

"Hallway to the Gods or some such," Nordic said.

He looked from side to side at the steep, sheer stone walls rising to his left and right, spaced about twelve feet apart. In each wall were colorful paintings of the sun, moon, stars, and broad, grinning or scowling, sun- or moon-like faces. They were the faces of the gods the ancients who'd once lived here worshipped or feared—probably both—and gifted with sacrifices. The ancient ones had told their stories on the walls on either side of the notch.

Their lingering presence was almost palpable.

Clara whistled, amazed, scanning both painted walls. "I've seen pictures like these before…but not so many in one place…"

Sunlight shone ahead of Nordic and then he and Clara led their horses into a broad, bowl-shaped clearing totally enclosed by rock walls. Tufts of grass and even a few gnarled cedars grew along the base of the curving wall. A shallow, crystal clear stream oozed out of a spring on one side of the bowl, ran through a shallow cut in the floor of the bowl to disappear into a small, dark hole on the bowl's other side. The ground here was littered with many chips of sun-bleached human bones—was almost paved with them—which told Anders this had been a place of sacrifice many thousands of years ago.

No doubt, they were human bones.

He slipped Apache's latigo and pulled the saddle from his back. "Good place to corral the horses."

Ten minutes later, leaving the horses in the bowl, clear of any possible flying bullets, Nordic and Clara walked back through the corridor with their saddle-bags, bedrolls, canteens, and rifles. At the mouth of the hallway, Anders stopped, surveyed the canyon below him, making sure it was safe, then turned and, crouching low, led Clara into the cave. Finn had followed them and now he ran ahead of Anders and into the cave, wildly sniffing the floor littered with recent bones of many shapes and sizes, some with fur still attached.

Likely, the cave had been a temporary home to predators of several varieties—wolves, wildcats, fox, maybe even a few bears over the years. The air was dank and bore the heavy, sweet odor of wild things and death. Still, it was a good place for a man occasionally, too—except for the nightly, ghostly howling of the wind. At least, he'd thought it was the wind…

"Let's settle in," Nordic said, dropping his gear and sliding his Yellowboy from its scabbard.

Soon, the two were lying belly down near the cave mouth with their rifles. Finn lay up close beside Nordic, the human who'd become not only his close companion but his security blanket, as well.

Nordic studied the narrow gap on the far side of the broader main canyon. Their stalkers would have to ride through there, in plain sight, if they were to gain access to the canyon. They might have been amateurs, but they were likely out there, just beyond the mouth of that narrow gap, smart enough to be wary of an ambush. It would have been a good place for one. They'd likely wait to make their move until shadows filled the gap. Possibly, depending on how eager they were to take down their quarry, they'd wait until dark to ride through it.

Something told Nordic they were eager, indeed. Something told Nordic the vengeance-hungry rancher and banker had offered them good money for the heads of Anders Nordic and Clara Vaughn. Dempsey and English were both likely trembling in their boots. Or, in the banker's case, brogans. They knew now what Nordic was capable of. They knew now they'd grabbed the tiger by the tail…

He and Clara waited, watching the canyon entrance.

Time passed.

Shadows slid around the canyon, growing.

After a couple of hours, Clara said, "You sure there's not another entrance to the canyon?"

"No."

"Wonderful."

"I've overnighted here before and scouted around a bit. I didn't see anything."

"Even tinhorns can stumble onto another access route."

"Don't get your bloomers in a twist, an' keep your eyes skinned."

Clara gave a caustic chuff and rolled her eyes.

More time passed.

Shadows filled the canyon.

Beside him, to his right, Clara sobbed.

Finn looked at her, whining.

Anders looked at her, too. Naturally, her aunt was on her mind.

He kissed her shoulder. "Sorry, honey."

"I can't believe she's dead. Just doesn't seem real. She was so *alive*."

Anders's usually stoic heart broke for her. Guilt racked him. If he hadn't come here, Maggie Rae wouldn't be lying in a cold grave under rocks.

Finn slid his snout up close to Nordic, sniffing, gauging the situation. He sensed the raw emotion here. Dogs were smarter than most humans gave them credit for. Finn was especially smart as well as intuitive. The dog gave his tail a thump against the cave floor then yipped softly and lay his chin down against his crossed paws.

He was a keeper, Anders thought.

More time passed.

The sun sank in a painter's pallet of vibrant mixed colors in the west.

The first stars shone weakly, gradually growing in vibrancy.

A coyote howled distantly. Finn lifted his head abruptly, sniffing, ears twitching, recognizing the voice of a distant cousin.

"Maybe we're wasting our time," Clara said. "Maybe they're not coming. Maybe they're heading back to town for drinks. All four are regulars at the Painted Lady."

"Could be," Anders acknowledged. "We've waited this long."

Clara looked at him and hooked a wolfish smile. "You're not just trying to get me alone in a cave again, are you? Never knew a man who liked passing the time with a girl in a cave."

Nordic smiled.

Clara leaned over and kissed his cheek and rubbed it in with a gloved finger. "I like passing time with you anywhere."

Again, Nordic smiled.

"If we get through this, you'll be leaving, won't you?"

Anders nodded.

"Figured as much."

"Maggie told me not to break your heart."

"Well, you just did."

"No worse than I just broke my own."

Again, she sobbed. "Listen to me. I haven't sobbed this much since my first cat died."

"I know how you feel."

"You don't think it would work?" Clara raised her brows. "You could help me run the ranch. You an' Finn."

Finn already knew his name. Hearing it, he gave an inquiring whine.

Nordic turned to her and, drawing his own mouth

corners down, shook his head.

He returned his gaze to the canyon that grew darker by the minute.

Presently, a howling sounded to his left. It sounded like a man dying.

"What in holy blazes is that?" Clara asked under her breath, pressing her shoulder up against the big man's.

"I heard it before," Nordic said. "I think it's just the wind building and passing through the corridor leading to the clearing."

Again, the howling sounded. Now it sounded like several men dying hard. Maybe a woman or two included. Nordic had heard it before, but it still gave him a shiver. The eerie sound dwindled to silence only to rise again a minute later.

"Good god," Clara said. "I don't mind sayin' that plumb scares me to the bone."

Nordic chuckled. "Sounds like the ghosts of those ancient folks sacrificed in that clearing back there…as though they're calling for someone to help free their souls."

"Dammit, Nordic," Clara said, punching his shoulder. "You're not helping!"

Finn turned to look toward where the howling rose sporadically, and mewled softly, apprehensively.

"I think I'd like to get out of here now," Clara said. "Take my chances with those four jaspers."

After another such howling blasted out of the corridor, Finn suddenly turned his head to peer into the canyon again. He pricked his ears and growled.

"What is it, boy?" Nordic said.

The dog continued staring into the night-dark canyon.

A minute later, distantly, interrupting the canyon's dense silence on the heels of another windy howl—or was it, indeed, the cries of the ancients who'd died back there?—came a soft thud and the clatter of a stone rolling.

A man cursed softly.

Nordic tightened his gloved right hand around the neck of his Yellowboy and slowly, quietly racked a round into the action.

"Showtime," he whispered.

CHAPTER TWENTY-THREE

Again, Nordic and Clara waited, especially tense now, the howling coming once every minute or so.

More time passed slowly.

"They're not going to come up here," Clara whispered in Nordic's ear. "They're either as scared as I am, or they know it's a trap."

Anders nodded. "I may have set a trap for *them*. But they know it's a box canyon. Now, we're trapped, too."

Clara scowled at him in the darkness, her hazel eyes glistening with admonishment in the starlight. "Nordic, this is not your first rodeo."

"I underestimated them."

"Knowing who they are…normally as dumb as hammers…I never would have figured them on figuring it out, either."

"You're just tryin' to make me feel better." Nordic raked a gloved thumb along his jawline. "Well," he said, slowly gaining his knees, "if they're not going to come to us, I'm gonna go to them. You stay here." He turned to the dog who'd started gaining his own feet. Anders placed a hand on Finn's head. "You stay with Clara, Finn."

The dog settled back down on his belly and looked up at Nordic, giving a soft, acknowledging mewl.

"I need to go with you," Clara whispered, after that stomach-churning howl came and went again, sounding like a thousand tortured ghosts. "I'll cover your back."

Nordic shook his head. "They're more likely to see two shadows than only one in the darkness. One can move more quietly than two."

"Are you sayin' I'm clumsy?"

Nordic placed a firm hand on her shoulder then rose to a crouch and stole quietly out of the cave and pressed up against the ridge wall on his left, hoping the darkness of the formation concealed him. Holding the Yellowboy down low by his side, so starlight didn't reflect off the receiver, he stood watching and listening.

No shadows moved on the slope before him.

His four stalkers must be hunkered down somewhere, probably at the base of the slope. Probably near the mouth of that narrow gap that gave access to the broader canyon.

Crouching low, Anders moved to his left and at an angle down the slope, quartering toward larger rocks on that side of the declivity. He got behind one of the rocks and then continued straight down the slope, moving quickly from rock to rock, waiting to move only when that eerie howling sounded from the top of the slope behind him.

He'd just moved quickly to the concealment of an especially large boulder—as large as the line shack—when he stopped suddenly and pressed his right shoulder against the slanting side of the rock. He dropped to one knee. He'd just spied a shadow move ahead of him in the darkness. The shadow grew as the man moved toward him.

At least, Nordic hoped it was a man and not a man-hunting wildcat.

Suddenly, the shadow stopped. Starlight glinted off what Nordic assumed was a rifle as the man turned to look behind him. As he did, Anders hurried forward toward the end of his covering boulder and stepped sharply right, into a gap in the rocks between his boulder and the one his would-be attacker was on the other side of. He took three long steps forward and pressed his shoulder up against the side of the boulder on his right now.

He stood there, holding his Winchester straight up before him, waiting.

Gravel crunched beneath a stealthy tread.

The crunching grew slowly louder before the man —tall and thin and wearing a cream Stetson with a stamped silver band—appeared in front of Nordic. The man stopped suddenly, started to turn toward Nordic. He gave a sudden grunt of startlement just before Anders smashed the butt of his rifle down hard against the man's head.

The man grunted again, dropped his rifle, and fell like a fifty-pound bag of cracked corn.

He lay groaning softly, writhing, grinding the heels of his spurless boots into the gravel of the slope.

Nordic dropped to a knee beside him and closed his hand over the man's mouth, squelching his grunts and mewls.

Shoving his face down close to the face of the man before him, Nordic said quietly, "Where are the others? Tell me or I'll crush your skull!"

He removed his hand from the man's mustached mouth.

Enraged eyes glinted at him. "Go to hell!"

Nordic raised the rifle again and slammed it down, crushing the man's skull.

A rifle thundered behind him. The bullet ricocheted off the boulder to his left.

Anders threw himself forward and over the man he'd just killed. He rolled up behind the boulder the dead man had just appeared from behind as another bullet slammed into the side of it, fast on the heels of the rifle's wail.

The wind—or those ancient, agonized souls—wailed once more…

Nordic's own rifle wailed, and he saw the shadow of the man who'd fired at him drop.

Rifle in one hand, Nordic leaped to his feet and ran down the slope, along the side of the stream on his left, in the shallow cut it had carved over the eons. When he gained the base of the slope, he climbed up out of the creek bed and moved slowly toward the mouth of the narrow corridor that gave access to the broader canyon.

Here the dark was especially dense. He felt as though he were wandering around at the bottom of a deep well.

He moved slowly, one step at a time, extending the rifle straight out from his right hip in that hand, holding his left hand out to one side, letting his fingers brush across the sides of boulders and spindly tree branches. He stumbled over rocks several times before another bullet curled the air off his left ear, followed closely by the flash and thunder of a rifle ahead and to his right.

Nordic stopped, took the Yellowboy in both hands, and sent three quick rounds caroming toward the flash of the rifle that had sent the bullet toward him, nearly tearing his head off his shoulders. The whipcracks of his own rifle were followed by a shrill wail, the clatter of a dropped rifle, and the thud of a body striking the ground.

Behind him sounded the ratcheting click of a pistol being cocked, a man's deep-throated voice saying, "Hold it, Dakota."

Nordic froze.

The man was so close behind him he could smell the cloying odor of sweat and tobacco, the oil of the revolver held close to the back of his head. A hand reached around Nordic and wrenched the Yellowboy from his hands.

"I'll take that."

The man tossed the rifle onto the rocks, making

Anders wince at the abuse of his prized possession. The man jerked Nordic's Colt from its holster and tossed that also into the rocks. Next, the man threw Anders's knife away.

He heard the smile in the man's voice as he said, "On your knees, Dakota."

"Go to hell."

The man smashed the butt of his revolver against the back of Nordic's head. Nordic stopped to his knees, sagging forward, wincing against the throbbing, burning pain in his skull. Again, the man smashed the butt of his gun against the back of Nordic's head. The pain lightninged through Anders's body, from the top of his head to the tips of his toes. He fell forward on his face and lay groaning.

His attacker lowered his head to within inches of Nordic's left ear. "You listen to me," he said, tightly. "We're gonna go see Mr. Dempsey. Alive, you're worth a thousand dollars. Dead, eight fifty. The difference ain't enough for me to take chances. So, you'd better be real—"

The man stopped abruptly.

Loud, angry growls rose, growing louder until the man above Nordic said, "No…now…you…*ahhh*…*ohhhhh*!"

Then Finn was on the man, slamming him to the ground and tearing into him, growling and snarling like a feeding wildcat, the man screaming and crying and sobbing and begging for mercy.

Finn gave him none until a slender silhouette

stepped up beside Nordic and Clara said quietly, "Finn, enough…"

The dog retreated from the man he'd attacked.

There were two loud rifle blasts, and the man's sobs went silent.

Still lying with his face against the ground, Nordic smiled.

———

E arly the next morning, Gentleman Jim Ridgely stopped his paint stallion and studied the steep, rocky slope before him. As he did, he puffed his ubiquitous, long cigarillo.

He could see two bodies—men clad in ragged trail gear—sprawled across the base of the slope, at the end of the long, slender canyon that gave access to the main one in which the steep ridge rose toward a cave at the top. Gentleman Jim put his horse up the slope and soon found two more dead men—one with his head caved in and a golden eagle feeding on his exposed brains. Another may lay nearby with two bullet holes in his chest and a badly mangled arm. Two buzzards fought over him, barking like dogs.

Gentleman Jim had heard the shooting the night before, as he'd been out scouring the mountains for his quarry, and having ridden late, was looking for a place to camp. That these dead men were the handiwork of the Nordic from Dakota there could be little doubt. Soon, he'd know for sure.

Gentleman Jim did not begrudge the raptors their

meals. Carrion eaters had to eat, too. He did not inter-
rupt them but went riding back out the slender canyon
toward the forested mountain country beyond. It didn't
take him long to find the prints of two horses that had
left the canyon.

They were heading south, into the high country.

Gentleman Jim smiled, tapped ashes from his cigarillo, and began following the tracks. They were not
easy to follow. Obviously, the Nordic knew how to
cover his trail.

But Gentleman Jim was an expert at following
difficult trails.

Soon, he'd locate the Nordic's cabin and earn a
healthy reward from the sissy Reginald English, which
would finance a winter for Gentleman Jim in Mexico
where he'd frolic with the *senoritas*. He puffed his
cigarillo and smiled at the notion.

———

That same morning but a little later, Aidan
Dempsey rode into Cimarron and pulled up to a
hitchrack fronting the Painted Lady Saloon.

Dempsey was not a happy man.

After all, he'd lost two sons who'd admittedly been
no great shakes but had been the fruit of his loins, just
the same. Not only had he lost Dave and Lon, but he'd
lost all of his men to one man.

One cussed, big, blond giant of a killer from
Dakota.

Now Dempsey had to build a new payroll.

To that end, slouched in humiliating defeat, he swung down from his saddle, slung the reins of his cream stallion over the hitchrail, stepped up onto the boardwalk fronting the watering hole, and pushed through the batwings. All eyes turned toward him, blinking against the heavy cloud of tobacco smoke. It was midmorning, but the Painted Lady never closed its door. Dempsey could tell from the watery brightness from the men's eyes—gamblers, drifters, drifting gunmen, former cowhands, even a former Pinkerton and stagecoach shotgun messenger—that these men had likely been drinking and gambling all night.

They weren't much but they'd do for starters. Dempsey could not tend his herds himself.

The saloon had gone silent the moment the rancher had entered. Of course, all the men here, as unwashed as some were, knew who the rancher was. Dempsey was the largest, most respected rancher in the area. He stood before the batwings, scanning the room, counting heads. There were twenty-three men and three scantily clad, sleepy-looking doxies, one sitting on the former Pinkerton's lap.

"You men know who I am," the rancher said huskily. "I need to fill my bunkhouse. I will offer each of you thirty a month and found to sign up right here, right now."

They glanced at each other then looked away, returning to their drinks and pasteboards.

Anger rose in Dempsey.

"Did you not hear what I said?" he fairly shouted.

"You know I'm good for thirty a month and three squares a day."

A couple of the men before him turned to him. One, the former stagecoach messenger named Lou Riley, said, "We also know you're good for getting your men killed, Mr. Dempsey. Uh…no offense."

Another man said, "I already have three bullets in me. I think a fourth would finish me off, and I'm only twenty-three."

He returned to his card game.

The fire of fury blazed in Dempsey. He hardened his jaws and ground his molars. He clenched his fists down low by his sides. He was ready to pull his .45 and start blasting away. Obviously, these men had no respect for their betters. It wouldn't do any good to shoot a couple, however. These unwashed rannies had made up their minds.

Stiffly, Dempsey turned and pushed angrily back out through the batwings. He stood on the boardwalk and looked around for other men he might be able to recruit. But the ones he looked at pulled their hat brims down low and looked at their feet as they passed the rancher.

Dempsey cursed bitterly under his breath.

He was exhausted, enraged, and humiliated.

He ripped his reins from the hitchrack and, still cursing, swung up into the saddle. He spurred the cream stallion into a ground-tearing gallop down the street and out of the town, heading back into the mountains.

He'd ridden for nearly an hour before goose bumps

rose along his spine. Dread touched him. He looked around for its source when, high on a rocky scarp to his left, he saw a big man sitting an Appaloosa with a dog sitting on the ground between him and a woman on a long-legged bay.

Maggie Rae's niece. Both she and the Nordic stared down ominously at Dempsey, the dog with his tongue out and ears pricked.

"Oh my god!" Dempsey said, terror building in him.

Staring back at the man from Dakota, Dempsey thought he saw the man smile.

Coldly.

Threateningly.

"Oh, Christ!"

Dempsey reined the cream around and put him into another hard gallop, his heart thundering in his chest.

CHAPTER TWENTY-FOUR

After ten minutes of hard riding, following a two-track trail through the sun-dappled forest, the rancher again stopped the horse and looked behind him.

Nothing but the pines, firs, and sun-blotched trail.

But he knew the Nordic and that damnable dog and woman were behind him. He could sense them in his bones. He had to get off the trail. On the trail, he was too easy to track. Panic rose in him. Somehow, he needed to follow the man who, once he caught up with his quarry, would make good on his promise to kill him. Dempsey had no one to back his play. He'd always had men to back him. Now, he was alone.

He'd never felt so vulnerable.

He swung off the trail and galloped along the shoulder of the slope, weaving through the trees, tossing frequent, desperate, horrified glances behind him. He swung the stallion to the right and rode up and over the crest of the ridge and down the other side.

War Bonnet Creek was at the bottom of the canyon below. He'd put the stallion into the creek, fouling his trail and losing his sadistic pursuers.

The cream galloped down the slope then whinnied and stopped abruptly.

Dempsey glared down at the horse. "What the hell are you stopping for, you cayuse?!"

Then he saw the two riders and the dog move out from behind a broad-stemmed pine.

They stopped to sit as they had before, the dog sitting between the big blond Dakotan and Clara Vaughn, all three pairs of eyes on him, regarding him blandly now.

The cream fidgeted, frightened.

Nordic and the woman and dog sat staring at Dempsey unmoving.

The rancher tried to say something, but no words would come.

He'd never felt this kind of fear. Before, he'd been afraid of no man. Of course, he'd had gunmen backing him. His broad chest rose and fell with his frightened breathing.

"You'll be hunted," Dempsey said when he finally found the words. "You'll be hunted to the end of the earth. They'll know who killed me!"

"Nah," the Dakotan said. "I have a feelin' no one gives a crap about you."

Dempsey swallowed. Fear was a wild stallion inside him. Finally, he rose in the saddle and barked, "If you're gonna do it, just do it and get it over with!"

Nordic said, "I'm gonna give you a chance. You have five seconds…"

"One…"

The rancher's fearful eyes grew wide as saucers.

"Two…"

The eyes grew wider and his big, broad face turned crimson.

"Three…"

Suddenly the rancher lowered his hand and snapped up his .45.

Before he could get it leveled, he heard the echoing bark and felt the bullet shatter his breastbone. He screamed, flew off the horse, and struck the ground with a heavy thud. He looked up at the big man and the woman and they both drilled two more rounds into him.

The last thing he heard was his stallion's whinny and the thudding of its hooves as it swung around to gallop back in the direction from which it had come.

Dempsey didn't hear the dog bark victoriously nor see it come over and lift its leg on him.

———

As Nordic, Clara, and Finn crossed the stream and started up the bench beyond which lay the line shack, Clara said, "Is it over?"

"It's never over."

"I didn't mean the trouble."

Anders looked at her, frowning curiously.

"I meant us, Nordic."

He drew a deep breath. "I'll be leaving in the morning." He kept his eyes on her as they approached the cabin, Finn running ahead to chase the rabbit that had been drinking out of his tin water pail on the humble shack's small, front porch. "I've attracted enough trouble."

"You should let your head heal. You took quite a braining."

Clara had wrapped his head, battered by his assailant's pistol butt, with a length of a cut sheet she used for bandages.

"I have a hard noggin."

"You're taking Finn?"

"Of course."

"You'll take a dog, but you won't take a woman."

Nordic reined up in front of the small stable flanking the cabin. The fading light glinted yellow and crimson in the breeze-brushed leaves of the cotton-wood flanking the stable. "Finn has nowhere else to go. He has no one but me. You have a ranch to run, five hundred head of cattle."

They swung down from their saddles. Again, Clara sighed as Nordic drew open the stable door. "Not going to be the same around here without you, Nordic."

He laughed at the irony of the remark.

When he was gone, the Chamas might know peace once more.

She winked, knowing what he was thinking. She flicked his hat brim with her index finger then rose on the toes of her boots to peck his lips. As she started to draw away, he placed his hands on her shoulders, drew her back to him, and kissed her properly, long and passionately, the way she deserved. She loved him, and he'd never been loved by a woman before just as he'd never loved a woman.

The last thing he wanted was to hurt her. Just as he didn't want to be hurt.

But there you had it.

Love…

He could no more settle down and settle in for longer than a few months than he could turn the cottonwood's leaves to gold.

"I'm sorry, Clara," he said, releasing her shoulders.

"Oh, shut up." She led her roan into the stable.

When they'd fed both horses hay and buckets of oats—they'd watered them at the creek and would take them down to the creek to water them again later—they went around to the cabin where they found Finn lying in front of the stoop, tearing at the dead rabbit he clamped between his paws, growling as he chewed.

Clara chuckled as she mounted the porch. "Well, we won't have to worry about his supper, I reckon."

They went inside and started their own, Nordic chopping at the haunch of the deer he'd shot recently while Clara cooked beans and a wild onion for stew. The cabin's windows dimmed. Clara lit a lamp and hung it over the table. Outside, birds piped in the gloaming and the breeze whispered, combing the trees. Nordic and Clara worked quietly with slow, sad purpose, not saying anything. Finn sat outside the cabin's open front door, curled up, nose to tail, snoring softly.

They ate, sitting across from each other, in the same brand of quiet which they'd prepared their meal. The windows were black. The breeze had died as the last light had bled out of the western sky, between silhouetted ridges. Finn had come in and lay down on the hemp rug fronting the closed door, again snoring softly into his tail, content.

They'd nearly finished the meal when Finn lifted his head from the rug abruptly, looked at the door, and growled.

Nordic had just taken a sip of his coffee. Now he set his cup down and regarded the dog curiously. "What is it, boy?"

Still staring at the door, Finn growled again. He looked at Anders and growled again, his nose working, ears pricked, signaling that trouble was afoot. Anders closed the curtains over the window behind him, rose from his chair, and turned down the wick on the lamp over the table.

"Stay here," he told Clara.

He grabbed the Yellowboy from where it leaned against the wall by the door.

"Who could it be?" Clara asked. "There's no one left."

Anders remembered the banker, English. He'd probably sent another would-be killer. His pockets were deep.

"We'll see," Anders said, racking a round into the Winchester's action.

Holding the Yellowboy up high across his chest, Nordic stood beside the door, caressing the rifle's cocked hammer with his thumb. A moon was rising, and faint, pearl light angled through the window to his right as he faced the kitchen.

A whizzing rose, growing quickly louder until it was followed by a *ping!* as the bullet broke through the window, caromed over the table, and thudded into a cabinet door. The bark of the rifle—a large caliber—thundered, echoing in the night.

Clara gasped.

"Down, Clara!"

He heard another thud as Clara dropped to her knees.

Finn snarled and barked.

"Finn, get away from the door!"

He'd no sooner given the order and Finn had sidled away to lay on the floor of the great room part of the cabin, than a bullet tore through the door, sending slivers flying in all directions, making nearly a fist-sized hole.

"Clara, you and Finn stay in the cabin!"

"Nordic, your head!"

"Solid wood!"

Quickly, Anders opened the door, stepped onto the porch, and drew the door closed behind him. He knew from the report the rifle was a Sharps Big Fifty and that it would take a few seconds for the shooter to reload the single-action rifle. He ran across the porch to his right and, despite his aching noggin, hurled himself over the rail and landed in a shrub. It was a soft enough landing. There was another eerie warbling sound then the bullet slammed into a log of the cabin to Nordic's left.

Anders had seen the rifle flash atop the bench before the cabin.

While his assailant ejected the large, spent cartridge and seated a fresh one, he sent three .44 rounds toward the crest of the rise then rose and ran quickly off to the cottonwood on the cabin's south corner. The shooter must have seen him because the next round slammed into the bole of the tree with a heavy thud and spatter of flying bark. The man was on the bench fronting the cabin, all right, likely hunkered behind the large rock that topped it.

Inside the cabin, Finn barked again.

Clara yelled, "Finn, get away from the door!"

Nordic ran to his right and around an old, wheel-less supply wagon nearly buried in brush. He dropped behind a gnarled cedar and waited for the next shot. He didn't have to wait long.

The bullet went *plunk!* as it tore into the cedar. The rifle went *boom!*

The violent din made his head throb. Fortunately, he was good at sucking back pain. He'd had plenty of practice.

Anders rose quickly, sent three more quick rounds toward the bench, and went running around the end of the bench atop which the shooter was bearing down on him. Nordic intended to work his way around and get behind the son of a bitch with the Big Fifty. He counted the seconds in his head since he'd left the cedar and dove behind a hummock of ground at the base of the bench, on the creek side of it as another large-caliber bullet blew up grass and dirt a few inches behind his right boot, the thunder of the Sharps reaching his ears a second later, just as he struck the ground and rolled to cover, gritting his teeth against the ringing in his ears from his battered head.

He raised his Yellowboy and sent three more quick rounds hurling toward the crest of the knoll, where he'd just seen the flash of the big rifle. After his third bullet had left the Winchester, he heard a shrill *ping!* He grinned. His third bullet had struck the Big Fifty's barrel. The man atop the knoll cursed softly. Anders heard a metallic rasp as the ambusher reloaded the Sharps. Two seconds later, another bullet blew up dirt and grass on the lip of the hummock of ground behind which Nordic had taken cover.

The throaty report of the rifle was still echoing when Anders rose quickly from behind the hummock and took off running toward the creek, tracing a zigzagging course, making himself a hard target.

Before he reached the creek, two more bullets cut into the ground around Nordic and then, as he splashed through the night-dark water glazed by the pale light of the rising moon, the water flashing silver around his shins, two more big bullets splashed into the creek to each side of him. He gained the other side, climbed the low bank, and ran into the forest beyond, another bullet hammering the bole of a pine to his right, only inches off his right ear.

He angled to his left as he ran up the low slope,

weaving around the pines. When he was a hundred feet beyond the river, in the protection of the forest, he held up behind a ponderosa, pressing his back against and edging a cautious look back in the direction of the creek. He knew the man would follow him. He was too determined not to.

English must be paying him a pretty penny to bring Nordic's head to him in a sack.

The notion made the big man smile.

Pressing his back up more tightly against the tree, holding the Winchester barrel up in front of his chest, thumb caressing the cocked hammer, Nordic waited.

Five minutes later, he heard water splashing softly. His ambusher was in the creek. Nordic couldn't see him. He was downstream to Nordic's right as Anders faced the forest sloping up in the darkness before him.

The night was quiet, the only sound the soft murmuring of the creek.

Nordic dropped to a knee and looked across the shoulder of the slope.

Time passed slowly.

Then there came the sound of a twig snapping under a man's stealthy tread.

There was another…another. Then the man's silhouette appeared to his right and down the slope maybe twenty yards. The man stopped. Moonlight glinted off the pistols in his hands, which would be faster for up-close work.

Anders picked up a rock and tossed if straight across the slope to his right.

The shooter's pistols spat smoke and flames in the direction of where the rock had thudded to the ground.

Nordic stepped out away from the pine, and the Yellowboy roared three times, loudly, the bore lapping orange flames.

His hunter grunted and fell backward, striking the ground on his back.

He lay writhing and grunting, grinding his bootheels into the forest duff.

"Son of a…son of a bitch!" he said.

Anders walked over to him, stood over him.

"Well, well," Anders said, gazing down at the tall, very thin man clad in a black suit and burgundy foulard tie. "Gentleman Jim."

He'd never met the man, but he'd heard him described. An odd, thin, specter-like figure. When he'd first heard the notorious Big Fifty roar, he'd figured his hunter was Gentleman Jim Ridgely, one of the nastiest regulators west of the Mississippi. The moniker was ironic. There was nothing gentlemanly about Jim except possibly the way he clothed himself. The man was clutching his chest with his black-gloved hands. His teeth shone white in the darkness as he stretched his lips back away from them, still writhing, grinding his heels into the ground, glaring up at Nordic.

"Nobody…nobody kills…*Gentleman Jim…!*" he cried, his voice girlishly shrill.

Anders aimed the Winchester down at the miserably groaning figure.

"I just did," he said, and drilled a .44 round through the killer's right eye.

EPILOGUE

Anders woke early the next morning.

He'd merely dozed intermittently all night, troubled by the knowledge he'd be leaving the beautiful young woman soon and troubled by his own solitary nature, as well. As much as he wanted it to work out between them, he knew himself well enough to know it wouldn't.

It couldn't.

Oh, for a few months, maybe. But then it would be even harder for him to leave. Harder for them both.

No, it was time to go despite his promise to Maggie Rae he wouldn't break Clara's heart.

The woman lay naked beside him, under the bearskin, on the shack's small, homemade bed. She'd rolled up against the wall, her back to him, as though even in sleep she was preparing herself for his leaving.

Nordic rose quietly, dressed quietly, Finn watching from the rug fronting the door which owned a fist-sized hole from Gentleman Jim's Big Fifty slug. The

dog watched Anders from where he lay on his side, a
skeptical cast to his eyes. He made no sounds, instinctively knowing Anders didn't want to awaken Clara.
Anders wanted to slip soundlessly out of her life,
making it easier for them both.

He stepped into his boots, wrapped his shell belt
around his waist, shrugged into his sheepskin-lined
buckskin jacket, and grabbed his rifle from where it
leaned by the door. He donned his hat, glanced at
Clara once more, then placed his hand on the door-
knob, saying quietly to Finn, "Let's go, boy. Real
quiet-like."

He tripped the door latch.

Clara's voice stopped him, husky with sleep. "No
goodbyes, eh, Nordic?"

He heard the bearskin rustle as she turned to him.

He glanced back at her. Her sleep-tangled hair
obscured her eyes. "No goodbyes," he said.

She turned her mouth corners down. "Farewell."

He nodded then opened the door and he and the
dog went out onto the porch. He stood there a minute,
his back to the door, squeezing his eyes closed as he
listened to her sob.

Finn mewled sadly, cocking his head as he stared
incredulously up at the big man, his only friend—a
man he understood to only a point.

As Anders did himself.

Just to a point.

————

Two hours later, Nordic rode into Cimarron trailing his packhorse, Angus, upon whose back Finn rode, regarding the busy world of humanity around him distastefully.

Anders bought trail supplies at one of the town's two mercantiles, filled his panniers, then swung up onto Apache's back once more and continued north along the busy main street roiling with dust and teeming with loud, unwashed humanity. He couldn't wait to be out in the tall an' uncut again, sipping one of his own, as-yet-to-be brewed, dark ales along some churning mountain stream. He was halfway through town when he checked his horses down abruptly.

A familiar figure had just stepped out through the batwing doors of the Who Hit John Saloon. Reginald English, clad in his impeccable three-piece business suit and crisp bowler hat, outlandish walrus mustache glinting in the lens-clear morning light, crossed the boardwalk fronting the saloon, waited for a break in the traffic, then, puffing a fat stogie, crossed the main street to the bank.

The dapper, self-important popinjay—the man whose devilish son had teased Finn with a stick, the man who'd sicked Gentleman Jim on Anders— mounted the boardwalk fronting the Stockman's Bank of Cimarron, took a final drag on the stogie before flicking it into the street, then pushed through the bank's front door. Anders heard the bell over the door ring, and then the door closed and the president and owner of the bank likely assumed he was safely inside, soon to be ensconced in what was likely his nicely appointed office…

…likely waiting to hear back from his hired killer, Gentleman Jim, as to the fate of Nordic himself.

Anders smiled.

He booted Apache forward, tugging on Angus's halter rope, Finn perched like a canine prince atop the panniers, ahead along the street. He waited for a break in the oncoming traffic then angled over to the tidy, brick bank. He stopped both horses, dismounted the Appaloosa, and tied both mounts to one of the three hitchracks fronting the Stockman's.

"Stay, Finn."

Hand on the butt of his bone-gripped .44, Nordic went into the bank.

Still sitting on Angus's packsaddle, Finn regarded the bank skeptically, canting his head this way and that, curiously, expectantly twitching his pricked ears.

After a couple of minutes, nearly drowned by the din of the busy town around the dog and the horses, came a man's screeching pleas for mercy followed by the quick roars of a .44. A brief pause in the gunfire was filled with the screams of the bank customers and employees and then there was one more, final gun roar.

A minute later, Anders Nordic stepped out of the bank amid the rattle of the bell over the door. He moved casually, a look of supreme satisfaction on his blue-eyed, blond-bearded face.

He paused to remove the three spent shells from his .44 and to replace them with fresh from his shell belt. He holstered the revolver, snapped the keeper thong in place over the hammer, then removed the reins of both his horses from the hitchrack, stepped up onto Apache's back, and reined both horses into the street, booting Apache to the north once more.

"Come on, fellas," he said. "I don't know about you, but I've had enough of this perdition."

Atop Angus, Finn gave a single bark of eager agreement.

Atop Apache, Anders Nordic, the big man from Dakota, put the loud, smelly town behind him and aimed for the distant horizon, heading he knew not where, just far from here and the stench of death while knowing that wherever he landed next, there would be trouble.

No matter how much he wanted…or thought he wanted…to avoid it, there would be trouble.

Or, deep down, did trouble make him feel more alive than peace?

If so, he need not worry. As sure as love would break a solitary man's heart, there would always be trouble.

A LOOK AT:
THE COMPLETE BLOODY JOE MANNION SERIES

WITH THE DUSTY TREAD OF WELL-WORN BOOTS, A ROUGH 'N' TOUGH HERO IS PRIMED TO UNLEASH HELLFIRE IN THE NAME OF WESTERN JUSTICE.

"Bloody" Joe Mannion is a town tamer of great renown—his temper just as famous. Recognized as the most uncompromising lawman on the Western frontier, he's a town marshal in the heart of Colorado Territory.

From bringing law to unruly towns in Kansas and Oklahoma to taming the wild streets of Del Norte, Mannion faces down outlaws, corrupt ranchers, and the darkest corners of the frontier.

But as the noose steadily tightens around Mannion's neck and bullets draw nearer, he reacts the only way he knows how—with a storm of bloody violence.

"The next Louis L'Amour." —USA Today **bestselling author Roseanne Bittner on Peter Brandvold**

This complete nine-book collection includes *Bloody Joe, Revenge at Burial Rock, Saints and Sinners, To Make a Man, All My Sins Remembered, Kicked Out with a Cold Shovel, Drawn and Quartered, Battle Mountain,* and *Bloody Joe's Last Dance.*

AVAILABLE NOW

ABOUT THE AUTHOR

Peter Brandvold grew up in the great state of North Dakota in the 1960's and '70s, when television Westerns were as popular as shows about hoarders and shark tanks are now, and Western paperbacks were as popular as *Game of Thrones*.

Brandvold watched every Western series on television at the time. He grew up riding horses and herding cows on the farms of his grandfather and many friends who owned livestock.

Brandvold's imagination has always lived and will always live in the West. He is the author of over one hundred lightning-fast action Westerns under his own name and his pen name, Frank Leslie.

Made in the USA
Middletown, DE
30 September 2024

61783283R00156